B. B West

Half-hours with the millionaires

B. B West

Half-hours with the millionaires

ISBN/EAN: 9783743372818

Manufactured in Europe, USA, Canada, Australia, Japa

Cover: Foto ©Andreas Hilbeck / pixelio.de

Manufactured and distributed by brebook publishing software (www.brebook.com)

B. B West

Half-hours with the millionaires

HALF-HOURS

WITH THE MILLIONAIRES

ARRANGED AND EDITED

BY

B. B. WEST

LONDON

LONGMANS, GREEN, AND CO.

AND NEW YORK, 15 EAST 16TH STREET

1892

CONTENTS.

HALF-HOURS WITH THE MILLIONAIRES.

——o;ⲟ;oo——

CHAPTER I.

MR. TWYGGE'S EXPLANATION.

My editor, a very high class editor, had com-
missioned me to write a series of vacation articles
on millionaires. Though I lived then on the edge
of Camberwell, where one might expect to find
them, it so happened that I knew of none there.
So I went to the city to pick up materials. I
thought that I should breathe them in between
Lombard Street and Founder's Court, if only I
kept my mouth open wide enough. Somehow I
did not. London is not like Paris, where you
have but to go to the Café de la Bourse, and pick
your millionaires by watching who eat most sauce.
Hereabouts they are secretive.

I was feeling a little disappointment and perplexity, which were new sensations to me, when
I was jostled off the kerbstone by my old ac-

quaintance Higgs. My own name is Twigg, or rather I should say Twygge, Stanley Marmion Twygge. Higgs was just the man to put me on the track; not exactly himself a millionaire, being an outside broker, and therefore the more likely to know all about the kind. I told Higgs what I wanted. "Yes," he said, "but the sort?" I replied .that to me any millionaire would be interesting. While I should prefer a collection of several, — say half a dozen, — two or three, if there were no more handy, would satisfy me. "Half a dozen," said Higgs; "that's not the difficulty. London is not like your beggarly Paris; the hard thing is to choose. Millionaires! The place is full of them. Do you like them in -son? There's Johnson, and Jackson, and Thompson, and Wilkinson. In -ris? There's Morris, and Dwarris, and Norris, and Harris. You can hardly stir without knocking against them. You must define."

I said I had no idea they were in such plenty. Any would do who could be induced to explain how they had made their money. Higgs gave a long whistle. "A very different thing that," he said. "They won't and they can't. Men are too busy, and too crusty, and too suspicious, while they are making their millions, to be bothered

with talk. When they have made them they
forget all about it. Shall myself, I dare say.
Besides, it is such stupid work. All the same
galley-slave jog trot, which nobody cares to
remember about. Sorry I cannot be of use. If
you had been asking how they spend their millions when they have them, I could have done
something for you. But the past-millionaires
don't spend their time here. They just come once
a week or so to draw their guineas at the boards
they sit on."

It was the very thing, I said, which I wanted.
Could he not introduce me, I asked, to a million-
spender. "With the greatest pleasure," was the
answer. "Come next Sunday afternoon to my
place, 10 Clancey Gardens, and I will take you
to Bob Hogson close by. He'll be glad enough,
I warrant, to see you."

CHAPTER II.

THE HOUSE-BACK REFORMER.

I KEPT my appointment, you may be sure, and after a glass of sherry off we went. We stopped a quarter of a mile away at a little stuccoed house, rang a wheezy bell, and were asked to walk in. Mr. Hogson was sitting in a dull dining-room, with a print of Ramsgate Sands on the wall, before a table covered with plans and estimates. He received us as civilly as if he did not know what to do with his time and himself, and began talking with grateful fluency about the weather. Higgs stepped in to the rescue. "I thought, Mr. Hogson," he said, "I might venture to bring my friend here. He is interested in millionairing." "Everybody must be," I said. "I should be deeply obliged, sir, if you would tell me the amazing story of your rise to your present proud position." "Just red herrings; not bloaters," was the answer, accompanied with something like a yawn. There was a pause, and the interview appeared in danger of dying of inanition, when Higgs again interposed. "Of course, of course,"

4

he said; "all the world knows that. But Mr. Twygge was curious to hear how you employ your little pile." Mr. Hogson's sleepy eyes opened then. He became almost animated.

"You see," he said, "when I had realized on the herrings and had parted with the fried fish shops to a society of Chelsea æsthetes, who still run them, I did not comprehend in the least what I was to do with myself. Not that I was worse off than any other millionaire. When you have made your million, it is easy telling yourself you only have to enjoy life. How are you to enjoy? Were you ever taught that behind the counter? Well, one dusty afternoon I was riding on the North London Railway, for the sake of something to do, from Kentish Town to Haggerston and back, second class, — I never go third, from principle, — when I looked down a whole row of backs — backs of houses, I mean. At once I felt a flash of light, somehow as if a fellow had hit me a smart tap on the head with a brick, or a gin-bottle. For a moment I was stunned, though I got better soon. I have been told I had a slight stroke, what is called, I believe, an idea. Very upsetting, but rather pleasant. At all events, I saw my way to spend money. Straight home I went. There is a handy fellow I know; brought up an architect.

Never lived by it. Was always fiddle-faddling, drawing, and doing things for himself, not hiring other brains. Next morning I sent for him. 'Come along,' I said. We walked to the street round the corner — a much finer place than this; rents four times mine. Rang a bell. Servant first thought I came for the water rate, and was civil. Was let into the hall. Took to thinking I was the plumber, when we went right through a passage into a sort of yard — garden, they call it. There I stood, and made my man look the whole back over as carefully as if it were Westminster Abbey. 'Give me a plan,' I said. We returned through the house. Footman still fancied I was the plumber. 'Shall be here again next week, and shall want to see your master,' I said. 'Drains?' inquired the man. 'What you like,' said I, and off we went.

"Next week my architect was here with as pretty a little picture as ever you saw under his arm. 'That's the sort,' said I. We went into the identical house, and through it into the yard. After a minute or two the master of the house came to us. 'Sanitary inspector, I presume.' 'Out again,' says I, 'except that your house, anywise its back, is a nuisance, and I will not stand it. Look at it yourself. A decent enough place in front; at the back ugly as sin. Look yourself. Do you call that an agreeable thing for a respectable man to have to stare at? What right have you to annoy me by forcing me to look at it from my back windows?' He was a reasonable kind of man, and allowed it was a miserable sight. 'But I,' he pleaded, 'never saw it in my life before. I never come in here.' 'You have no right,' said I, 'to vex your neighbours. It is more aggravating than a range of pig-styes. How much will you take to let me put it right for you?' I called to my architect to show his plan for a reconstruction of the whole back. My neighbour liked it, or did not dislike it, and I did not quarrel about terms. A cheque of mine was soon in his hands, and a troop of workmen was carrying out my architect's instructions.

"We made a good piece of work of the business. A pretty conservatory was rigged up, and a closet window was turned into an oriel. I ran trellis traceries all over; planted Virginia creeper everywhere, and inserted a bit of red-tiled roof. The rest of the £200 tenants in the terrace were frightened by my energy. They knew I should be upon them if they did not stir themselves. Every back was transformed, except one which was in Chancery. There I put my men over the wall, and we settled it without asking leave. Somebody got an injunction when all was finished. What of that? I flatter myself there is no handsomer front view than is the back view of Dewery Terrace."

That seems to have been only the commencement of an enterprise which has transformed London, though Londoners are hardly aware of the fact. Mr. Hogson had, like all busy men, certainly an ample command of leisure, and he bestowed a good share on us. As he very fully explained, it was not all plain sailing for him. In the beginning his visits were commonly resented as an intrusion, or a trespass. Often he had to flatter and wheedle his way in. He would apologize and say that his eye had been caught by an ingenious chimney-stack, an ornamental balcony, spout, sanitary pipe, or what-not, as he was looking out of his friend Mr. Smith's back attic window. He asked leave to examine it with his architect. His architect, when he came, reported it admirable, only it would be so much better with a slight change of elevation. The owner, if he consented, was lost. Hogson, once in possession, could not be dislodged till the entire premises were double-fronted.

The pill was sweetened by the absence of anything to pay. On the contrary, Hogson would one day bring a box of elaborate bricks, architectural, — all house backs, — for the children ; or a landscape — back — of Nuremberg, for the mother. The workmen were provided with packets of best Assam to mix secretly with the kitchen tea, which naturally they partook before quitting work. Hogson himself never went his rounds without a cheque book in his pocket. His difficulties, he told us, were much greater with the poor than with the rich. Not rarely an artisan had a taste, with canons which were not Hogson's. If there were to be an alteration, he wanted it carried out after his own way. Sometimes he had found a beauty and picturesqueness in the disorderly chaos. Oftener, with a load of family cares upon him, he was impatient at being worried with rich men's crotchets, as he thought them. Among the refined and prosperous, on the other hand, there was a fair sprinkling of persons whom the novel excitement amused. To them it was like a first reading of Ouida in a dissenting household to have Hogson enter, with a few Persian tiles, a fragment of marble balustrade from the palace of the Capulets, or a pot of honeysuckle, to break the bleak untidiness, the horrid prose, of the incoherent zigzag. Two large families of daughters of Irish viscounts have been known actually to call and thank the millionaire for the indulgence of his whim.

Even in ill-to-do quarters he boasted to us that of late he has ceased to be severely repulsed. His visits in streets where backs have remained backs begin to be expected as decrees of fate. "So here you are at last, Mr. Hogson," is a common if sulky greeting. The occupant feels it is hopeless to resist, though he gives no sign that he is obliged. His main object is to extenuate and attenuate. With his wife and sons he will go about the yard, and point out that the windows are not nearly so much out of harmony as at the end of the terrace. When, as not rarely, Hogson has encountered intelligent people as obdurate as the most stolid, he has found it feasible to barter an improvement in the row which backed theirs for permission to improve their premises. At times he has had to call in his lawyer to draw up distinct contracts for mutual easements of embellishment.

The function he has assumed has dragged him, he told us, into the oddest complications. One family did not live at the back, having enough rooms in front, and was obstinately indifferent to the advantage of a prettier prospect or retrospect. Mr. Hogson was in despair till a happy thought occurred to him. He had learnt that an eligible young man with a taste resided in the backing terrace. Him he brought acquainted, at a picnic arranged at infinite trouble for the purpose, with the young lady of the perverse household. They fell in love, and she took to haunting the back window, which had a view of the gentleman's house. A process of unconscious attraction drew him to the same side. His eye was offended at the unsightliness of his goddess's shrine, and she worked upon her father. Rather ungraciously he assented to Mr. Hogson's prayer to be allowed an entrance. Both backs were metamorphosed together. Mr. Hogson, who had presented the bride with a magnificent diamond brooch, had to be fetched by main force to propose the health of the young couple into the breakfast-room, from the yard, where he was found revolving as if on a pivot, in dumb admiration of his architectural panorama.

The reform is, in general, not of a kind to advertise itself. You have to pry into mewses, or ride along suburban railways without a newspaper, to be properly disgusted at the unfathomable ugliness of the backs of London houses. But there it is. It is a brooding misery to the maid-servants, who consume a substantial portion of their day in

gazing, duster in hand, and yawning at it. It
oozes right through the tenements, and is present
in a latent and demoralizing way to busy men, as
they stare up at creditable fronts. I have said:
" There it is." That happily is a mistake of the
tense for persons with eyes, as, on quitting Mr.
Hogson, with hearty thanks, I soon discerned.
As I peered round street corners, and through
casual gaps, I arrived at the surprising knowledge
that the town is no longer what it was, in respect,
at any rate, of its backs. Mr. Hogson's million is
bearing fruit. Where there was once the most
odious deshabille in brick, now there is fair regu-
larity, or picturesque irregularity. Mouldy, sooty
yards have been converted, sometimes, into ver-
dant terrace gardens, with parterres and fountains;
sometimes, when individualism has been too per-
tinacious, into graceful little Cordovan patios.
You may come upon a square of fresco, a patch of
mosaic, on a wall. It may be a statue on the sky-
line. It may be a glowing little window conservatory. Some spot of beauty everywhere, at
short intervals, is discoverable, as any reader of
that fascinating but rare and costly volume, " London Backs, by Rudolf Squheacher," will speedily
understand.

Not that the old dreariness does not die hard in

places. I lighted on a very odd instance the other morning. I was smoking a pipe in East's study in Gibraltar Gardens, when I noticed a most deplorable back opposite. "Monstrous," I cried, "that in these days a nuisance like that should be tolerated, — the one blur in as pleasant a backscape as can be seen. Whom in so respectable a neighbourhood as yours can it belong to?" "Atrocious, I admit," was the answer. "But what can one do? A poor old creature lives there, who can scarcely keep body and soul together, to judge by his coat, much less do decorative improvements." "All right," said I; "just tell me his name, and I'll find somebody to do them for him." "Oh," said East; "Pogson, or Hogson, or something of the sort."

I had wanted an excuse for renewing my acquaintance with Mr. Hogson; and I had it. I determined to go at once, and inquire how it was that charity did not begin with him at home. He was in, but not at all in a mood for a joke against himself, though willing enough to have an audience for his wrath. "I have been robbed," he cried; and I began to condole with him on the loss, as I presumed, of spoons or a family teapot. "Worse by far, a hundred times worse," was his reply. "There are pirates about, sir, pirates. When I had done with my backs, I had always intended to take up the fronts, of course. What do you think, sir? There is Prough, the stupidest blockhead even among us. Have you seen what he is doing? I caught him staring one day at my backs. 'No poaching, Prough,' I said. 'On the contrary,' said he, 'I was admiring, not envying.' He put it in a sort of inverted commas way, I am sure I don't know why. Only, I knew he was up to no good. When people talk like that, they never are. Well, what do you suppose I next heard? Positively he has sneaked a license from the County Council, and has bought up the rights of all the ground landlords and occupiers on the route, and is running a boulevard from the Bank, throwing in the Finsburies, down the City Road, by Gray's Inn Road, Euston Road, Marylebone Road, and Oxford and Cambridge Terraces, and Sussex Gardens, with side aisles to Regents Park, slap into Hyde Park. But I'll try for an injunction, for a *Quo Warranto*, for a *Ne Exeat Regno*, for anything, if there be justice left in England!"

"At any rate, a fine idea," I remarked. "Fine idea!" shouted Hogson, growing black in the face. "Should think it was, indeed. But 'tain't his. Mine, mine, and I would have fried fish a dozen years longer to be the man to bring it out. Had been just going to apply for the concession, when this brute cuts in. Besides, he can't do it. No taste, no nothing. And the grandest thing in London to be christened 'The Prough.' Bah! Here's a country for you, where a man cannot keep an idea to himself. I shall emigrate." I did not poke my little bit of fun at Mr. Hogson about his neglected yard, and I let him talk: I always do let millionaires; but I cannot say I object so much to Mr. Prough undertaking the improvement while I am alive. London backs are enough for one man. A millionaire should not be a dog in the manger.

CHAPTER III.

I HAVE no regular house. My plans of life are not yet formed. Some time or other I may go in for a million myself, which makes it a little hard to decide how I shall permanently live, and where. Meanwhile I do not like to tie myself up too closely. So I lodge about here and there. Occasionally I favour the airy north-west. A mile off is a famous common, bright and breezy, outside the gates of the great smoke wall. A common they call it, and so a bit of land thereabouts really is. But the secret of its charm is in the open spaces all round, which are in private ownership. Lately the old man to whom they belonged died. He had chosen to retain them unchanged. He was pleased to feel that he kept open a lung of London. But he had only a life estate, and his heir on the whole prefers cash to his uncle's sentiment. He is no curmudgeon. He has not been asking a full building-land price; only a fair advance on the agricultural value. The London municipality was always prepared to

16

give the bulk of this. So it said; but the economists inserted a condition that the local vestry
should raise a fifteenth part, being reasonably sure
that the vestry wouldn't.

Last June the vestry was to vote, and I
attended, in the gallery. Being a lodger, I was
anxious that the rate-payers should be liberal
to their uttermost farthing. That was not the
view of the meeting. From the speeches I
discovered that the parochial householders con-
sidered London much in debt to them. They
would, if possible, exclude Londoners at large,
and especially those of the adjacent parishes,
from their playing-fields. They would, if they
could, admit none but the bonâ-fideyest of trav-
ellers, and allow them none of a bonâ-fide's
drinking or brass-band privileges. The demand
of a local contribution to the purchase naturally
appeared to them a shameless attempt at extortion.
Real justice, it was clear they thought, would be
done only if they were appointed conservators,
and authorized to charge gate-money. A resolution, rejecting the County Council's invitation in
peremptory and almost offensive language, had
been read by the chairman, a leading local jerry-
builder. He expressed his hearty personal con-
currence, scoffing incidentally at the notion that
a brickfield could be an eyesore, or nosesore.

The motion was on the point of being put, when an elderly man, shambling and shy, rose in the body of the hall, and began brushing with his sleeve his hat the wrong way. I easily saw by his coat what he was; and the name which the chairman respectfully announced to the meeting, confirmed me. Mr. Richard Shanks agreed cordially with the prevailing opinion, as I should have anticipated. Millionaires do not like rates, and they see no reason why a community should need other lungs than private deer parks. Mr. Shanks, however, to my surprise, except that millionaires are entitled to be eccentric, reached the orthodox conclusion somewhat singularly. His speech was long, because he obviously had not the art of cutting it short. He alluded to the mode in which he had become a millionaire. He had been a shirtmaker, and, by shaping the armpit gore rhomboid instead of oval, he managed to save several square inches of material in every shirt. If you manufacture enough, every rule of arithmetic, except common subtraction, proves you must thus in time become a millionaire. Mr. Shanks manufactured enough, and the result followed.

"So you see, gentlemen," he proceeded, as if he had been enunciating a syllogism, " I am not likely to differ from the resolution — in principle. Still, in fact, there is a way out of it. The £20,000 we are at liberty to subscribe is, of course, not worth talking about. Any one here would be much too glad to be permitted to volunteer a cheque for the amount. I propose that the names of intending donors be put into a hat, and that the one drawn shall be accepted straight off for the total." Thereupon he held out his own hat, and, after putting in a wisp of paper with his name on it, beckoned to the beadle to carry it round. Finally, it was taken to the table, where the chairman, finding no other paper inside, declared Mr. Shanks the successful candidate for the duty, and tendered his warm congratulations. The winner briefly expressed his acknowledgments, wrote a cheque for the sum, and the meeting separated.

I was interested, as I always am, in millionaires, whom I should like to keep in phials, and put from time to time under a microscope to watch the process of decomposition into fluid gold. Following Mr. Shanks out of the hall, I offered him a velvet brush for his hat. I always carry one when I attend a public meeting or conjuring exhibition. He was gratified by my courtesy, and willingly entered into conversation. I told

him of my researches into the natural history of
retired millionaires, and said I should be happy
to include his experiences with the rest. He was
flattered by the compliment, and described to me
his system. "In the first place," he said, "do not
let there be any misunderstanding. You think you
see Mr. Richard Shanks. Now, I am really not
Shanks, a single gentleman; I am a company, a
syndicate. For myself I have a mere couple of
millions, let alone a few pocket pieces hidden away
somewhere against a rainy day, which I conceal
from myself. My pittance would not go far, if
there were nothing else. But there is John Stalk-
eye's little pile, and Nehemiah Fisher's, and Wig-
gles's, and a heap of others. We are the Put-
London-on-its-feet syndicate, with me for managing
director. When we had settled down we resolved
not to fritter away our little competence. We
were going in for big things, and on a big scale.
We would not be squandering like Partridge, who
thinks his million and a half well bestowed in giving this or that lame dog a wooden leg. We don't
care that for individuals. Partridge" —I made a
mental note of Mr. Tobias Partridge's name—
"is always compassionating the sorrows of widows
and orphans. Widgeons and ortolans, say we.
Pity the sorrows of the whole community, is our

motto. We must, we know, draw the line some-where. Now, charity should begin at home, and we draw the line at the bills of mortality.

"Our search is for things London wants, our London, the London which has made us, and for the things it cannot afford itself. Had your sleep broken lately by steam whistles! No? Thank the syndicate. We found people did not venture upon prosecuting, and that the vestries would not. Too many steam whistles are vestrymen. So we lived up and down the town, and prosecuted wherever we lodged. All as still as mice at last. Where did you say you were staying? Haverstock Hill at the bottom. Maréchal Neil roses bloom there freely—do not they? That is our millions. In Camden Town nobody would apply the Smoke Abatement Acts. Instructed my solicitor. The three railway companies and the twenty-five facto-ries laughed in his face. 'How do you like,' they said, 'three courses and dessert, *Nisi Prius* with one Judge, Division with two, Court of Appeal with three, and House of Lords, to wind up?' 'Very much,' answered my Mr. Dodges; 'and better still if you could make room for a rehearing or two. Mr. Shanks—' 'Eh! Shanks? That alters the case,' they remarked one after the other. 'Yes; will stop smoking, if we may send over to

Mr. Shanks's sanitary engineer to execute the necessary alterations.' Of course, we never object to that. Saves trouble and expense in the end, doing things the right way at first.

"I hope you like the avenues from the Marble Arch to Charter-house Square. We planted them. The parishes too poor. That was an expensive job, but well worth doing, the putting the telegraph and telephone wires underground. The Post Office, you remember, really could not afford it, though it sulkily admitted the advantage after the Permanent Under Secretary for the Home Department's head was taken off in the March storm three springs back. Even then the Secretary to the Treasury was very uncivil in the matter, and raised an infinity of objections to our outlay. Almost a more troublesome business was getting leave to dig subways from Hamilton Place to the opposite gate in the Green Park — the crossing on which the two historians, the newspaper editor, and the poet were killed last year — and from the Albert Hall to the Hyde Park side.

"Public authorities are the deuce when they ought to do something and won't, and one wishes to do it for them. You can hardly imagine the trouble I had with them and their snow. Everybody knows they never sweep the snow away in front of public buildings. Law not made for them, they say. Well and good; but it took me months before they would suffer me to clear it off for them at my own expense in front of the British Museum and the National Gallery. That I call dog-in-the-mangerly. We are persevering, however, and we win in the end always. There was the Buckingham Palace job, for instance. I dare say you do not recollect the old hospital façade, — a disgrace to the Kingdom. My partners and I determined to cure it. We had all the drawings prepared, and I took them in a morocco leather portfolio, with our architect in a brougham, to Windsor. Her Majesty saw them and us with her usual courtesy, and had the Premier and the First Lord of the Treasury in waiting. When our talk was over, she had them fetched in. As she stated, and they could not deny, the look of the place was discreditable; indeed, she had ceased to reside in London from dislike of the view as she returned from her drive. The First Lord began to demur to the proposed remedy, on the ground of expense. 'But,' said her Majesty with her gracious smile, 'I and Mr. Shanks, that is, Mr. Shanks and I, have arranged all that.' The minister could only grumble, and had to acquiesce.

"But I must not talk any more at present. I am due at the Mansion House at three. Nine-tenths of the London hospitals are insolvent. The town cannot supply the deficiency, and they come down upon us. I do not know yet how much they want. Whatever it is, they must have it. You say you hope all will not be used up in providing for the big jobs; that there are so many little ones which need looking after. Trust the Odds-and-Ends brigade for them. Teake is their man, you know. What? don't know Teake? You must know him. You see him everywhere; a shabby little old fellow, always dressed the same — trousers, coat, and waistcoat the same cut and pattern for the past dozen years at least. Be any night in the season by eleven at the fifth crossing in Eaton Square, and you'll find him sure enough. Bye bye; I shall be late at my meeting, but they will wait for me, I fancy."

CHAPTER IV.

THE ODDS-AND-ENDS BRIGADE.

I REGISTERED mentally Mr. Teake's address, — rather a queer one, — and was on the spot at the time specified. It happened conveniently for me. I had just alighted off an omnibus on my way towards an At Home in Belgrave Square. As I respect the society of millionaires, I always by preference go to At Homes by omnibus. That is their way. But the crossings are an objection. Wherever you go you are intercepted by crossings; that is, by mud without crossings. I was speculating how I should ford the Marylebone Road of the South West without a speck on my boots, when, to my profound amazement, as I came to the margin of the slough of despond, there was a crossing, the neatest, driest crossing that ever brush made. It was as amazing, with its wall of mud on either side, as the piled-up Red Sea must have been to the Israelites. Over I went, and in such a fever of gratitude that I was feeling in the pocket where I keep my gold change for the penny I knew I should not find, to reward the sweeper, when on the further bank I saw Teake; for Teake I was sure it was. "Nothing to pay," cried Teake, as I went on fumbling in my pocket, not being certain if he were not expecting toll. He, as it was, confirmed the assurance of his own disinterestedness by extracting eighteen pence from a canvas bank silver bag he held, and handing the amount to a very unprofessionally zealous sweeper.

It never does to be shy with millionaires, who are seldom shy with you. So I introduced myself off-hand to Mr. Teake as a friend of Mr. Shanks who had spoken with admiration of him. "Hates me like poison," said Teake; "thinks me and my set wandering pirates. But you can't help that. What was it you wished to ask me?" In the first place, I told him that I should be glad of an explanation of his present employment. "Easy enough," said Teake. "You must know that every crossing-sweeper in London strikes work by five or six at latest, when he brushes the mud over his beat, and goes home to dinner. Now that the County Council has bought up the crossings, and emancipated the town from the nuisance of a horde of licensed mendicants, diners-out and at-homers who prefer walking are no better off. Between the hour at which the Council sweepers retire and the parish sweepers come on, there is an interregnum of unadulterated dirt. There was our chance; and we Odds-and-enders have undertaken the job.

"'How many of us are there?' I am sure I don't know. Now and then an Odds-and-ender scrapes into a regular place. Shanks, I have heard it whispered, did it, and, of course, he looks down upon his old trade. There is no saying but I might have done the same if I had been caught early enough after I made my million. But I was too old to wait for a vacancy, and now I like the odds-and-ends freedom. Vagabondish, perhaps, but amusing. We hunt round for the little gaps, and fill them. Plenty of screws loose to be found, if you are not too proud and particular to go tinkering. Here's this overtime crossing business. One of our clerks searches the Court Journal for the coming entertainments. Another musters a corps of casuals at the workhouse doors, gives them a good square meal, and marches them, dropping a man, broom and all, at each essential crossing. Then, from eleven to one, I trot about paying, and seeing that each is at his post. Have you never remarked that there is always a crossing, and that the man politely declines your pence? Why, it has been going on in Belgravia and Mayfair for a good couple of years."

I certainly had not noticed the phenomenon. The reason may have been that I have happened constantly to be pre-engaged when I have been invited by my friends in the two quarters. At all events, I was so much interested now that I took old Teake's arm, and offered to throw over my Belgravian acquaintances, and go the round with him. He was willing enough, and very communicative. London has no notion of all it owes to him and his fellow Odds-and-Ends men. Not one Londoner out of a hundred could say who turned Trafalgar Square into a flower garden, and relieved so many hundreds of police from attendance there, that a twelfth part of the London pickpockets have emigrated in despair to the Burmah ruby mines. The burglars have to thank Teake and Co. for something besides. It has been ascertained by the Statistical Society that eighty-six burglaries a year might have been nipped in the bud if the burglars had not heard the tramp, three streets off, of the policeman's boots. Scotland Yard has acknowledged it with tears in the Chief Commissioner's eyes. Could not be helped. Policemen cannot dispense with boots; and the Parliamentary vote is but just enough for two pairs of boots apiece at ninepence the pair with the creaks in them. Teake chanced to see two burglars, who had just prised a street door, shut it to without going in, till the constable had gone by. He called at the Yard the next morning, and had the figures reckoned. He walked over to the Home Office, and fought it out with the Under-Secretary, who had, at last, to give in, accept the cheque, and sign a fresh contract without creaks.

"What do you think," continued Teake, "of our cabs and the caballometer? Never have seen them, or it, you say? You don't ride in cabs? But you cannot have helped observing our cab paymasters. Fancied them new watermen, you say. A very different kind of being altogether, you will find. Once upon a time, to take a cab was something between pulling the string of a shower-bath in December, and bargaining for glass-bead necklaces in Venice. You were in for a commination service, or a higgling match. So, as the municipality would not or could not interfere, we bought up the whole lot. The four-wheelers we shipped out to the King of Dahomey, who, being, by treaty with France, precluded from slicing up his termagant Queens, required some more Christian-like and equally painful instruments of torture for their discipline.

Our Hansoms and patent broughams we have had fitted with caballometers. These record the length of the journey. As you descend, a slip of paper protrudes from the vehicle, with the fare in one or two dimensions. The same machinery locks the driver in his seat, and muzzles him, till the passenger has had time to be out of earshot. If the distance be close to the margin, the fact and inference are indicated by a hand signifying a *buona mano*. A passenger has the option of paying at the journey's commencement or conclusion through the paymaster.

" Probably you are not aware, that but for us the Government Offices on Jubilee Night would not have had a tallow candle of illumination. On the morning not a single band would have been playing. We heard in the nick of time of the neglect, and had fifty bands drilled to play in concert. Did not catch a note, you say ! None so deaf as they who won't hear. All I know is, that it was a lovely concert from ten to three. The best feature of the festival in some people's opinion. How intolerably dull it would have been, remarked one intelligent foreigner in my hearing, if the authorities foresooth had not wisely thought of this !

" But, really, of the presents to London upon which we Odds-and-enders have a right to value

ourselves most, the extirpation of the beetles counts,
I believe, first. It was nobody's business. So naturally it was ours. London allowed itself to be the
victim of a veritable nightmare, of which it might
have rid itself whenever it pleased. Only it preferred shuddering and groaning. We planted
ourselves in the breach. The insects, if they be
insects, reside happily and innocently for five
months of the twelve in their own homes within
the walls. Nobody minds them there. All which
was necessary was to persuade them of the charms
of domesticity during the remaining seven. We
set our retained men of science to work. Our
naturalist imported from Brazil the anti-blatta
devorans, which has the peculiarity of feeding only
upon cockroaches. But the expedient was voted
by us cruel. Why should beetles not live as well
as millionaires? We took passages back to Rio
for the a.b. devorantes. Fortunately our chemist
discovered a compound applicable to mortar, which
is the object the beetles issue from the walls to
seek outside in warm weather, when it fails within.
Since that has been used in house-building or re-
pairs, the beetles refuse to wander abroad. For
two years past such has been the dearth of them,
that Mr. Stevens last week knocked down a perfect
specimen, authenticated as of London growth, for

£3 15, after a lively contest between the representatives of two American museums.

"That," went on, after a pause, Mr. Teake, "was rather an important business. But life is made up principally of small things, and its pleasantness of small pleasures. So, I may be excused if, though I am sensible it is a matter rather of sentiment, I couple with it a very dissimilar enterprise, a certain minute job of my own of old date. I was in Stuccopolis one evening, glooming with a dull friend, an admirable man, when I heard a voice — such a voice — ringing through the night air. Both of us were in a stupor of stucco-stagnation; and the lethargy broke up as by the breaking of a spell. A thought came to me. I bid my crony a hurried good-bye, ran downstairs, caught up my hat, and pursued the voice. Three terraces off I came up with it, and, on some preposterous pretext, spoke to the singer. I had his history in a moment; a grocer curst with a singing throat, and no musical genius. Had been in the Bankruptcy Court through following his voice, which, with the drag of invincible native stolidity, could not lift him to the Opera or St. James's Hall. Clearly he was miserably out at elbows, gaunt, and dismal; with no intellect in particular, and no vice except that he liked lying in bed all day. A bargain was soon struck with him, £3 a week, and a holiday from August to the middle of September. His duty, I stipulated, should be to beat the bounds of Bayswater and South Kensington, warbling like a London nightingale, when the deadly full-fed dulness comes on, from 8.30 to 10.30. 'But the police?' he asked. 'They do not approve,' he complained, 'of night warblers': he had been in trouble already with them. Besides, the poor vagrant had learnt himself and humility. His compass was confined to a few notes, sweet though those were. He feared he should be ridiculed as an impostor when he stood singing before a house. I saw my way out of the double difficulty. He must pretend, I told him, to sell hard-bake, and his song would be a commercial hard-bake call. Let him carry a basket, and it would be enough. He might walk as fast as he pleased, and need not trouble himself about customers. The moment he is heard, up rush the maids, who have not been taught by experience, to buy; and the wandering voice is by the time half a mile away. I have only to reproach myself with having done a good turn to those drones the ground landlords. Rents on the round have risen twenty per cent., thanks to the evening voluntary.

"But good-night, young gentleman; I have

emptied my bag, and I have to get home to Holloway. It is a busy day for me to-morrow. A millionaire's time is worth nothing; yet he has plenty
to do with it. In the morning at eight I have
to arrange for a floral parade of orchids up and
down Paddington on the dull days from November
to April. At half-past I am to sign the agreement
with Blogg and Khirms — the two men, you know,
who keep the register of the weekly increase and
decrease of carbon in the planet Mercury. I have
agreed to buy their brains for two years at an
income of £3000 apiece. They will discover for me
a gas-escape detector, which I mean to present to
London. Mercury must wait for the measurement
of its carbon. Too bad to have the air poisoned
for four millions of people, and every house pulled
to bits once a year, because no gas-fitter can tell
you where precisely a leak is. At 9.30 I shall
settle about the lavender tincture for the water-
carts. At ten I am to be with the British Museum
Trustees. There is a lien on their vote. Unless I
give them a couple of thousand, the first Shake-
spearean folio, with the poet's own remarks on
Hamlet and explanations how Juliet has to dress
her hair, will be off to Philadelphia. At half-past
eleven I have to buy off St. Martin's portico from
the County Council's tender mercies. At two I

must be at the Auction Mart to bid for the garden
at Bayswater. I do not covet the ugly place; but,
if we Odds-and-Ends men do not take it, the builders will, and down comes the great cedar. At four
the ringers are to try the chimes at St. Clement
Danes, and I have to decide which bells are cracked
and will have to be refounded. At five I am
under an engagement with the Royal Water Colour
Society, as President of the True London Leaf
Green Revivalists, to watch that the Once-a-Week
Thorough Wash Brigade is properly cleaning the
Hyde Park elms; and at six I am due in Kensington Gardens to see the nightingales' eggs put in
the thrushes' nests, and the turf laid down in glow-
worms. How I am to find time for being present
at the opening of the dozen square gardens, which
the Brigade has taken advantage of the temporary
ducal depression to buy and throw open to the
sweltering public, with a free tea-table and music
in each from August to October, I cannot for the
life of me tell. Good-night, once more, good-
night."

I tried to stop him for a minute, in order to
express my lively admiration of the multifarious
kindnesses which in such delightfully confusing
profusion he was conferring on London. He was
fagged, however, with fourteen hours of hard work,

and took a gloomy view of the results of his benevolent exertions. " Dare say," he muttered, as he
shuffled homewards, " 'twould be much better if I
had let it alone. But one must do something after
bone-boiling for half a century."

CHAPTER V.

THE CHARITY-WRECKER.

THE other morning I happened to be at the Probate Office. I wanted to see whether my old friend Purkiss had really left me nothing, even by a revoked codicil. I had nursed his affection for a dozen years, at a frightful cost in boot leather, omnibus fares, and pretty speeches. He had neither wife, nor child, nor acquaintance, only me, and on me his money would have been well bestowed. No; the *Illustrated London News* and the *Times* had told the truth. Very ungratefully, he had divided the whole among half a dozen hospitals. It was of no use trying to prove him crazy, as I virtually believe he always was; for, not being even a tenth cousin three times removed, I could not have come in as an intestate's next of kin. My grandfather's widow — that is, my step-grandmother — had married Mr. Purkiss's brother-in-law's great-uncle. So I was in the habit of calling him uncle. But I understand he was not so, even in law.

However, that is not much to the purpose.

I had noticed that an elderly gentleman was waiting till I should have done with the will; and the supposition did not hasten my search. As I turned round, something struck me in his appearance. He had the shabbiness which to my senses — and I have an instinct — spells or smells of money. The coincidence that he should have been inquisitive about the same will was curious. I loitered, therefore, at the office door, though the messenger scrutinized me as suspiciously as if I were trying to coin the dust in the air into full-blown residuary bequests for myself. At last the unknown came out, with a look as if he had discovered something unpleasant. I thought he must be a member of the council of a rival institution to those which had defrauded me. He stopped short, and eyed me. "We were doubtless on the same quest," he said. "Could you have imagined Purkiss would have been such a fool?" After all, thought I, he may be no philanthropist, but only, like myself, a victim of misplaced confidence in human generosity or justice. The possibility comforted me, and I intimated something to that effect.

"No," he replied; "Purkiss did not know me from Adam; and I should not have cared for his money. I am a warm man myself, perhaps a warmer man than was he." "May I ask, then,"

I remarked, "what brought you here?" "Oh," he said, "I had to find out what charities he had chosen. The *Times* did not give the names. These extracts from wills contain just enough to tantalize, and no more." My estimate of the old fellow fell again. I guessed he was another lunatic on the lookout for a public charitable object, when there are so many worthy private charitable objects about. With a slight suggestion, I fear, of a sneer, I asked: "And to which of Mr. Purkiss's favourites do you, sir, intend to give a crutch?" "To none," he answered; "that is not my line; yet it is important to me to ascertain which particular charities are being enriched by these idiots." He saw I was intelligently and sympathetically curious, and gave me a card with an address rather respectable than affluent, in Bloomsbury. "Come," he said, "when you have an hour to spare. But it must be after four in the afternoon. I am busy till the Courts rise."

I had forgotten the engagement; for I had come to the conclusion that, in spite of his disclaimer, he must be a disguised charity tout, when one afternoon I met Higgs. He was coming out of a house in a west central square; and, as I shook hands, I suddenly recollected it was my casual acquaintance's address. My interest was excited, for Higgs visits none but millionaires. "I was thinking of paying a call here," I said. "Ah!" said Higgs; "there is indeed a millionaire with a head on his shoulders, who understands what to do with his money." I should have liked to inquire more particularly; but Higgs was in a hurry, as I often have found him to be. "You know him yourself," he said. "In with you. For the moment I am sure he is at leisure." I acted on the advice, rang the bell, asked for Mr. Bar- strow, the name on the card, and was ushered along an untidy passage into an untidier back study, with a view over a nailed-up pump and a dead poplar. Mr. Barstrow was sitting there, and he remembered me in a moment. "Sit down," he said, "and I will tell you all about it." I had asked him nothing, but he saw it all in my eyes.

"When," said he, stepping forthwith *in medias res*, "I made my million —." How, I inquired, inter- rupting. "Just like them all, I suppose," he said. "I have forgotten the details, the precise way, not that it signifies. I rather think I got leave from the Crimean government to dig up the dead chargers for my jargonelle pear drop factory at Whitechapel. Then I made a good thing of the bones for best ivory knife-handles." That surprised me, and I ventured to hint that horses' bones do not answer for the purpose, though human bones, as a cutler of my acquaintance has tested by small experiments, will. " Oh, ah," said he, a little impatiently, " horses' bones, men's bones — what's the difference ? " " And for jargonelle pear drops ? " asked I. " Why not ? " said he. " At any rate, my jargonelle pear drops sold famously ; they were noted for a specially piquant and pungent flavor. I turned the whole concern into a limited company, and got out with my million." — They all, by the by, say 'my million,' just as every Inspector of Schools is Her Majesty's Inspector. — " What, then, to do ? I am a plain man, with no expensive incumbrances, no wife and children. I know nobody but Higgs, and don't want. I looked round for an occupation, and found everything used up, except money-making. No vacancy for promiscuous benevolence — the whole chokeful. Private and particular munificence — engaged a dozen deep. If you have the art, solid and bonâ-fide, of painting, doctoring, chattering, inventing a new bottle-stopper, or a new gas, discovering a planet, picking pockets, lining your own, there is always room. For a millionaire there is no room."

" Try, you and your million, to squeeze in as a charity-monger, a connoisseur, an entertainer of Grub-street, as a dissolute roué, if nothing better, or a gambling turfite, and you will comprehend the tribulations and humiliations I have endured. You will soon understand that making your million is child's play to spending it. Ah! those were weary days when I first gave up the pear drops. Not rarely I felt like stealing into the factory with my master-key on a boiling-night, and dropping into the big vat a worthless millionaire to come out savory jargonelles. But I have hard core in me, and I bore up, though it was heart-breaking work. Fancy; at a promising institution's doors before they open, to secure a fair place in the queue. In at last, with a rush, and seated meekly on the edge of a chair in the secretary's room. 'Very sorry,' he says, 'but I am afraid I have no good news for you, Mr. Barstrow. You see you really have not been waiting long. Just cast your eye over the string of old candidates. Why, here is Baring-Coutts Smith; he sent me by Parcel Post a bundle of £1000 notes last week without any address, thinking I could not identify and return them. But our detective traced them at the Bank, and poor B. C. Smith bears the disappointment bravely.'

"I must confess I was not so heroic as B. C. Smith, or so ingenious, and I was in despair.

But one morning, when I had been touting round the Campden-hill studios for a rising Apelles to fatten up, I chanced to pass the gates of the Hospital for the Relief of Diseases of the Thyroid Gland. I turned in at the porter's lodge. My habit was to fee hospital porters on the off chance of early intelligence of vacancies in the list of £1000 donors. I inquired if there was any news. None, as I expected; but I was tired, as well as sore in spirit, and sat down. A patient came in for a parting chat. He had just been discharged. 'All right?' asked the porter. 'As right as a trivet, the thyroid,' said he; 'but hang my thyroid; what am I to do with myself? They have kept me three years curing the thyroid with clear turtle and dry champagne. What is to become of me? My home is broken up, my occupation is gone, I am fit for nothing but conger and the brut, as they call it; and pray, how am I to get them, even if I am taken on again as a journeyman carpenter?' 'That's what you all say,' answered the porter; 'seems rather ungrateful, don't it?' he remarked to me. I returned no answer, and did not stay to hear more. 'That's what they all say,' I repeated. I dare say, and I dare say they all say it at a hundred other institutions. An idea had dawned upon me. I had my vocation at last, and could bid haughty secretaries and supercilious committees for the selection of munificent benefactors go to Jericho."

"You are not to suppose," he proceeded, after a pause to suck up all the sweetness of the recollection of gratified vengeance, "that I began by publishing my intention to the charity world. On the contrary, I grew more diligent than ever in my attendance on philanthropy. But I approached it on a fresh side. I did not waste my time in importuning for liberty to be a donor. I became a committeeman, a very dissimilar personage. I had myself put on the boards of a dozen benevolent institutions, and by my emissaries watched as many others. Nothing has for years happened, nothing has been received, nothing been spent, without my being able to track it." "But what for?" I interpolated. "What for?" he cried; "what for? To baffle the charity-mongers, to countermine their cruel plots, and to rescue their miserable victims! It has been a colossal task, and one too long neglected. But I hope I have overtaken a good many of the arrears. Hundreds of the poor creatures, marred, persecuted, trodden down beneath the charity Juggernaut, I have managed to set on their feet.

"I commenced by letting it quietly be known,

through secret channels at my command, that I
was prepared to help the prisoners of charity.
One of the first to call upon me was a dilapidated,
mouldy creature, well dressed, and fluent of
speech. On a card which he sent in was printed,
'Mr. George Bracks, Hostel for Irremediables,
Larkspur.' He sat down by the fire, without an
invitation, in the easiest chair in the room, after
testing them all — my easy-chair, from which he
saw I had just risen. Then, having first asked
me to be sure to put his hat in a safe position,
and to shut the door, he told his sad tale. Before
he entered Larkspur, — the College, he called it,
— he had been managing clerk to a brewer, with
hours from seven to six. He walked to and fro
between his house and his office, three miles and
a half each way. 'Here is what I was in those
days,' said he, as he produced a coloured photograph. A bluff hale man was there represented,
with a rather bullying expression of face. He
had a hearty appetite, and plenty of energy for
his work. But it happened one morning, as he
was presenting an account at a surgery, that the
doctor saw his left hand. 'What is that?' asked
the doctor. 'What is what?' asked the clerk.
He glanced in the direction of the practitioner's
eye, and perceived it was bent on a minute pimple.

'A wart,' he remarked. 'No,' replied the doctor; and he brought out a glass to examine it. 'It is, I fear,' he muttered, 'a caricoid accretion. Does it not grow?' 'Really, I have not noticed,' answered the clerk. 'Do,' said the doctor; and off went his visitor, having forgotten to collect the bill for porter.

"From that hour all Bracks's thoughts were occupied by his pseudo-wart. He scrutinized it in church; he felt it at dinner. He counted it in his addition sums. He dreamt of it as elephantine, and woke up to measure it. His employers perceived there was something wrong. They couldn't help it; for his ledgers were all diapered with sketches of a monstrous excrescence. They were very friendly, and reasoned with him. They inquired if it pained him. 'No,' said he. They asked if it were an inconvenience to him in writing. 'No,' said he. Then they recommended him to take no more notice of it. That was easier said than done. Finally, they intimated with much concern that things could no longer go on thus, and they put him in a cab, and carried him to a distinguished surgeon. Sir Richard diagnosed him and the quasi-wart minutely. To the patient's mingled triumph and sorrow, he pronounced it no wart. It was not caricoid, but it was bound to increase, though gradually. In time it must grow as thick and long as his arm, if only he would live long enough. For perfection the excrescence required him to be a bi-centenarian. The great man did not anticipate pain, or even especial annoyance; only growth. Bracks might, in the course of a hundred to a hundred and fifty years, have to convey his fungus about in a go-cart.

" If the poor fellow had meditated on the affliction before, you may conceive that he meditated tenfold now. He developed unsuspected powers of fancy, and illustrated every account-book and business note with pictures of his finger as it had been, was, and would be. One afternoon the senior partner called him within his glass cage. ' My good friend,' said he, ' we cannot go on like this. We are as sorry as you; but business is business, and porter is not warts. With grief we have been driven to the conclusion that you are no longer a brewer, but an Incurable. We have been using our influence with the Committee at Larkspur. It has itself had an interview with Sir Richard, who is profoundly delighted, or rather, I should say, interested, by your phenomenal case. He is convinced that there is no remedy, being con-

firmed in his original opinion by the painlessness
of the ailment. Pain, as he reported to the Committee, is Nature's beneficent provision for com-
pelling the rest of an organism to insist on the
application of a remedy. Where there is no
pain the constitution gives itself no trouble in the
matter, and lets the malady be. The Committee
has become as fascinated by your case as Sir
Richard ; and here,' ended my excellent master,
' is your nomination. You are now and hence-
forth a full Irremediable.' ' I expressed my
thanks,' said Bracks, ' took the diploma, beauti-
fully emblazoned with the College arms, a skull
and cross-bones erased, packed up at my lodgings,
paid my few bills, and by the close of the week
was installed as a First-class Confirmed I.

' At first it was heavenly. No more getting up
by candlelight. No more trudging through Isling-
ton slush and sleet. I was a gentleman of leisure
and an independence, with all found. The medical staff was duly impressed by my case. It was
so curious to suffer by an affliction which did not
afflict. The chaplain continually cited me in his
sermons as an example of the mitigations of evil.
As he showed to demonstration, here was an incurable patient, who, alas ! could never hope to be
as other men, yet bore all without a groan ; in-

deed, would not have known what to groan at.
Meals were many, plentiful, and carefully prepared. There were pretty grounds to stroll in,
with anxious attendants at intervals of a hundred
yards, ready with wraps and umbrellas, if the sky
darkened. Above all, there was the blissful freedom — nay, encouragement — to reflect upon one's
disease. At the brewery I had succeeded latterly
in appropriating a fair proportion of the day to
that luxury. But my conscience — not that its
pricks were very acute — would remind me that
it was stolen time. Unseasonable interruptions,
moreover, came from the outer office, and the
somewhat inconsiderate glass cage. Here I could
fold my hands, the warty one uppermost, and
ponder peacefully.

'No wonder the fungus throve upon such diet.
I had been measured for it, and it was proved
to have, in my first collegiate year, increased
by a centi-millimetre. Meantime, however, its
host — that is, I — began to fade and shrink.
My flesh ever since has been falling away, and my
colour growing more leaden. I am being absorbed
into my fungus, which pampers itself at my expense. By a mere accident, sir, I heard of you. I
read the report of the Anti-Tintinnabulum Infirm-
ary v. Barstrow, in which you were the defendant,

with the evidence of the unhappy patients, restored by you, at the risk of an indictment for a criminal libel, to health and society. I made up my mind to see whether you would exert yourself to deliver me, too. Can you, and will you?'

"The man was conceited, lazy, and egotistical. He had been a ridiculous simpleton, who deserved his fate. Still, I could not but pity him; and I had an old grudge against the Committee of the Hostel for Irremediables. I promised him to do what I could, if he would be amenable, as, with tears in his eyes, he engaged to be. First of all, I directed him to apply for a furlough of three months, to nurse or bury his grandmother's aged aunt. As soon as he was safely away, I commenced operations. My solicitors, in his name, gave notice of his intention to resign. The legal gentleman who represented the Hostel replied by forwarding a copy of the contract executed by Bracks on his induction. By this it appeared that, in the nature of things, an Irremediable once is an Irremediable always. Clearly that was the logical construction of such an agreement, if the Committee wished to hold an inmate to it. They did wish it. But I was able to circumvent the obstacle. Forthwith, by arrangement with my late partners, —good-humoured, as all connected with the grease and confectionery trades are, — I set Bracks to superintend a sister candle factory. Nothing in his bond hindered him. He had to be up at three on boiling-days, and to be at work twelve hours at a stretch. The result was that his colour came back, and his flesh hardened. He grew stout and muscular, and acquired a tremendous laugh.

" At the end of his vacation, when he obediently reported himself, he was manifestly incapable of donning the Hostel garb which he had left behind him. A new suit had to be ordered for him, in which he looked portentously healthy and vigorous. Sympathetic visitors were scandalized by huge guffaws resounding from the quiet groves. The fungus itself had suffered. At the periodical measurement it was discovered to have seriously dwindled. The state of things was alarming. The head Physician communicated to the President, a Royal Duke, his forebodings that it might disappear altogether. No fiasco could be more deplorable. The sister establishments would not refrain from relating that an Incurable had been cured at Larkspur. In face of the consequent infusion of an element of uncertainty of mortality, the tender atmosphere of pity and resignation could no longer be preserved unbroken. With reluctant desperation the Committee eventually accepted an offer I made. All the cost of Bracks's maintenance was to be refunded by me with interest, and he was to consent to be cashiered as a healthy impostor. I was present at the ceremony when he was solemnly rung out of the brotherhood. All the Irremediables were ranged in a row, and a doleful company they were. Bracks would have made any three of them. His Irremediable cap and cloak were stripped off him; and out he stepped without a blush on his countenance, which was, in fact, too generally rosy to have revealed one, if any had tried to exhibit itself.

"My next enterprise was on a larger scale. You may have heard formerly of the Adoni-bezek Hospital. There was no such prosperous institution once. It was a special hospital, with a paid secretary, a paid medical staff, and everything proportionately handsome and expensive. Perhaps you do not recollect the sort of disease it was established to treat; not that such a detail is particularly important. Well, Adoni-bezek, as you will see in your Scripture history, was King of Bezek in Canaan, and had the habit of cutting off the thumbs and great toes of the princes he quarrelled with and subdued. Now, an ingenious practitioner in want of patients had ascertained that a joint of the thumb and great toe is subject

occasionally to a slight cartilaginous enlargement.
Some say it comes from tight boots and gloves.
No: they declared they did not mean a bunion;
far from it. There, at all events, it is. Whether
a person have it or not matters little, and it
requires some surgical acuteness to make sure that
it exists. Mr. Glumthorpe, F. R. C. S., possessed
the sagacity. Suddenly, no one knew how, a furi-
ous controversy arose in the medical journals. Mr.
Glumthorpe brought the light of science to bear
on the obscure malady, and one morning the
growth awoke to find itself famous.

"A meeting was held at the Mansion House. A
fund was started. The community became aware
that it contained thousands of afflicted *pollicaires*.
A good site was bought at a very good price; and
the Adoni-bezek Hospital rose, with an eminent
marquis and philanthropist in its chair, and an annual dinner, ball, and fancy bazaar. A learned He-
braist had no difficulty in rehabilitating the much-
abused King of Bezek. He proved, etymologically,
not so much from Exodus as from Hittite inscrip-
tions, that his Majesty was a physiologist in advance of his age. He kept a private hospital for
patients of high birth; and his operations on great
toes and thumbs had been mistranslated as ampu-
tations by the contemporary *Spectator*. While in

personal attendance on the inmates of his Home the good Prince himself caught the malady, and was operated upon for it successfully at Jerusalem.

" Nowhere were the agency's fees more liberal than at the new hospital, and its friends were proportionately zealous. The percentage was allowed to anybody who introduced a subscriber. Solicitors were promised a generous bonus if they produced a will, drawn up at their office, with a legacy in it for the Nib, or the Polly, as the place was variously and fondly termed. Preachers had an honorarium slipped into their overcoats after a charity sermon. There was a daily lunch on the premises for well-wishers. Patients were sedulously beaten up, and carefully kept. Never was such a bubble blown, and I resolved to burst it.

" The full incidents of the contest would take too long to relate. The Nibs and Polls fought for dear life; but I turned the Anti-Vivisection Society upon them. We stirred up to rebellion the patients whom we found kept with one thumb bound up, and one boot off, so that they should be disabled for honest work. We tempted them to run races, and play fives. An executor was prosecuted for accepting a premium on a bequest. I hired a rabbi to expose King Adoni-bezek out of the Talmud. Finally, I had the

entire asylum placed by the Court of Chancery
in charge of an official liquidator, at the suit of
a creditor for a hundred gross of patent Tor--
quemada thumb-screws, which he had supplied
and never been paid for. Sometimes I come
across an old patient. You may always recognize
the class by the little hole drilled in the side of
the thumb, if the glove be off, as it rarely is. It
is delightful to think of the rescue of the poor
creatures from a discreditable and indolent existence. Even the officials are conscious of the debt
they owe me. Last week I had a call from a man
whose short hair told a tale. He introduced himself as ex-secretary of the Adoni-bezek Hospital,
and gave a melancholy history of the dishonest
courses to which his experience there had led him.
But for me he might, he confessed, have been still
in that fraudulently snug berth. Nothing short
of my energetic efforts could have dislodged him.
Now, though force of habit had carried him into
various peculations, ending in Holloway, — not
one of the well-known philanthropist's foundations
— he was thankful to state that he was happier
than if he had been permitted to go on cheating
the credulous, and boring holes in able-bodied
great toes.

"There, sir!" Mr. Barstrow went on, "you have

two samples of my exertions — successful exertions
I think I may call them.   I could mention plenty
as remarkable, if I or you had time.   I might tell
you of several Cripples' Homes from which I
ejected the vivacious prisoners.   In my note-books
I have minutes of the happy breaking up of ten
distinct Orphans' Asylums, and the restoration of
the inmates to their numerous sorrowing relatives.
You should have seen me as I presented myself at
the Freemasons' Tavern on the morning of an
election to the Middle Aged Shrews' Refuge, with
more than half the voting-papers in my pocket,
and filled the vacancies with plump-cheeked,
cheerful dames, whose aspect frightened away all
intending subscribers, and drove the institution
into insolvency a year and a half later.   I have
not restricted myself too narrowly to the over-
throw of public charitable impostures.   My mission is to redeem the prey of a cruel beneficence of
whatever kind, the sufferers by expectations from
any other source than their own efforts.   Jargonelle pear drops with a hoofy, churchyardy flavour
never served a better purpose than when I was
inspired to apply in these directions my honourable savings.   Look at me, plain Jeremiah Barstrow, who, but for the luck of turning in at the
lodge of the Hospital for Relief of Diseases of the

Thyroid Gland one dusty summer morning, might have ended by being the mainstay of half a dozen pauperizing societies, and the absurd donor of numberless thousands of pounds from J. B.

"It was a very near chance. I never knew how near till I emptied out into the street the whole board of the Deceased Paupers' Next-of-kin-Expectancy Aid Corporation. Brigson snarled out at me, as he passed me when I was watching the disconsolate exodus of Patrons, President, Vice-Presidents, and Committeemen. 'A fine fellow you to triumph! We were within an ace of choosing you a £5000-Life-Governor five years ago. Where would you have been then?' But I was not elected, as you see, and here I am, the Charity-Wrecker. Good-morning. I am due at a creditors' meeting, *re* the bankruptcy of the Toothless Cats' Soup Kitchen."

CHAPTER VI.

THE NON-PAUPERIZING CHARITY-MONGER.

I OWED my introduction to another millionaire to Mr. Barstrow. As I was walking along the City Road, which I frequent when I desire a quiet and rural stroll, I came upon him suddenly at a street corner. He had a companion with him, and was evidently out of temper. As may be supposed, I accosted him, and looked so hard at his friend that he could not avoid introducing us. "Mr. Nathaniel Griggs," he said; "Charity Griggs, you will generally hear him called by our sort." Then he appealed to me on the topic they had been discussing. "What do you think of Mr. Griggs for a moral man?" he cried. "Nobody could have displayed finer qualities in the encouragement of self-help in his own case. Real rough-and-tumble, and the devil take the hindmost. Yet the instant he has mounted, down he kicks the ladder. A positive Charity-monger! All vile selfishness; fighting against the Past-millionaire's plague of ennui." Past-mill-mal, Mr. Barstrow styled it. "Even you, Twygge, would know better than that, if you ever had a guinea to give away. But I cannot stay to listen to any more sickly sentimentality. If I could send friend Griggs and his million into the Bankruptcy Court, I should consider myself a benefactor to him, and it and society."

He planted us there, and out of mere civility I had to stop with Mr. Griggs. I apologized for my acquaintance Barstrow's heat. Mr. Griggs assured me he was not hurt, for to a certain point he entirely concurred with Mr. Barstrow's feeling. Charity-mongering as a profession appeared to him simply detestable. Nobody could be more alive to the folly, for instance, of old Quaterstell, who every full moon sends a cheque for £2000 to the institution which on the day has a multiple of patients in its wards corresponding to the days of the month. "There is, at least," he said somewhat apologetically, "method in my madness. I seriously believe that I do as little harm as may be, if any." Mr. Barstrow had convinced me by his arguments of the depravity of bolstering up charities, and I courteously intimated my surprise at what seemed to me a paradox. I could not understand how a well-known philanthropist, as was Mr. Griggs, could help being, with the best intentions, as I was confident were his, a public enemy.

"I imagine, nevertheless," he said mildly, "that I have found a way, and I do not mind making you the judge.

"When I set up millionairing, everybody admonished me: 'Of all pastimes do not go into philanthropy.' I believed the warning to a certain point, and have always steered clear of charitable institutions. I myself go a step further, and have never wished to set up as a benefactor of the community. I think the community is a humbug. But I thought I might be safe in reserving my benevolence for individuals. At all events, there could be no great harm, I supposed, in fostering obscure genius. The only gentleman in my family had been an attorney's copying-clerk. So, out of regard for his memory, I searched the Inns of Court for briefless barristers of high promise. I admit I had to buy my experience, and rather dear. In other words, I made a mess of it. I soon discovered plenty of my sort. Generally they were hard-working, frugal, literary. Half a dozen of the number, if let alone, must have become eminent, provided they had not starved first. After twenty or thirty years of honest penury, they might, I dare say, have risen to the Bench or the front rank of journalism. Thanks to my protection they have crystallized into men of taste,

One, it is true, has escaped. He let all my gifts run through him as if he were a sieve. Throughout he remained as disorderly and extravagant as ever, with spells of real work, which will lead in time to Parliament and a Law-officership. But I am persevering, and I am sober-minded. I am not one of your bee-in-the-bonnet millionaires. I am not like Bogus, for example, who, after scraping together a bare million, has laid out half in the purchase of a Connemara property. He fancies he is improving it with the other half, while he lives on buttermilk and blunderbusses. I kept three principles steadily before me: not to make a fool of myself; not, so far as possible, to make fools of other people; and not to make fools of my pounds, shillings, and pence.

"I reasoned the matter out, and endeavoured to discover why I had failed before. I observed that the gift of a well-bound and most expensive copy of Alison's 'History of Europe' to my young nephew at Uppingham left him apparently as straightforward, not to say as blunt, a lad in the utterance of his views about his seniors as ever. A tip, on the contrary, of half a sovereign caused him to flutter about three aged female cousins, when he bade them good-bye before returning to school, with the air of a love-sick pigeon. The bequest of the most hideous house in South Kensington to my friend, the accomplished and fastidious Paterson, has not pauperized him. Yet Widow Brown, the hardest-working charwoman in the parish, has been turned into a begging letter-writer by election to the Bividuary Society's lath and plaster almshouse, with an allowance of half a crown a week, after the death of her second tipsy husband. Queckett was perfectly simple and unaffected after the *Saturday Review* mentioned that he would be a very pretty poet if only the sense of melody and thought in his last volume of verse had been at all in proportion to the high, moral tone discernible in it. Why did he go about with an inane simper on his face after the *Kettle-in-a-Hole Weekly Temperance Dreadnought* had bewailed the prostitution of an exquisite muse like his to the celebration of the charms of a glass of champagne foaming at the lips of beauty? At last I was on the true track. I had learnt how to enjoy the pleasures of philanthropy without the lamentable consequences of misanthropy. Just take care to give the playthings of your beneficence something they don't want, and they and you are secure. I mean, you must give them things which you know, and they don't know, are good for them. The moment they recognize that a gift is covetable, cease to give it. If they still want it, let them work for it.

"I commenced with a corner of St. Giles on my new method. Previously, in my ignorant inexperience, I had distributed a consignment of the best Spanish donkeys among the Mile-end costermongers. They sold every one to the sausagemakers, and turned casuals, till I should have over a second shipload from Andalusia. With St. Giles I was more artful. Nothing, I was persuaded, in all the life of Garden Court, great St. Andrew's-street, was so noisome, or ought to have been so intolerable, as the lodging accommodation. In seasons ordinarily prosperous the people had food, which, though indigestible for others, was for them fairly palatable and was abundant. They had their games — cudgels, and brick-bats; and their music — street debates, which opened the lungs, and enriched the popular oratorical vocabulary. With all this they were full of complaints, others than medical, about every luxury they relished most. Against their dirty, poisonous habitations I never heard a single charge.

" So. I bought up the Court, and pulled it down bit by bit. The ruins I replaced by durable, neat, rain-proof, and smell-proof tenements. These, room by room, I offered at the old rents to the ejected lodgers. They grumbled, and accepted the offer, because they had virtually no option. At first they combined to force me to lower the rents, on the ground of the extra expenditure on soap. They said they could not sit down comfortable and grimy in such fine places; they had to wash their hands, and sometimes their faces. I was obdurate, and had for a while a rough time of it whenever I put my head inside the Court. 'Have they not grown grateful?' you ask. Certainly not, unless cabbage stalks be the Garden Court equivalent for thanks. What is more to the purpose is, that they are much the better themselves for water, substantial roofs, and civilized conveniences. They do not know it, and thus their independence has escaped with the bloom upon it. Yes; they call me Crotchet Griggs, and admire their own amiability for humouring my freaks so far as to consent to live on my improved property.

"I do not pretend that I still did not commit blunders. Among my St. Giles acquaintances was a capital fellow, a carpenter. He did many honest jobs for me, and I was in the habit of talking with him. The object he desired most was the establishment of his wife in a little corner

general shop in Dyer-street. The premises were
to let, and he coveted them innocently but ar-
dently. One day I met him. He was almost
crying. I inquired the cause. 'Oh, sir,' he said,
'they have gone and let the shop. The bill is
down.' I walked back with him to the spot.
'Yes, indeed,' said I; 'the notice has been pulled
off. Ah, and the door has a name over it.' My
friend followed my eyes, read, and stammered out,
'My wife's name! what can it mean?' 'Simply,'
answered I, 'that I am your landlord, and you
are my tenant. Fetch your wife at once, and see
that the stock is all right. I intend to have tea
with you. The fire is burning in the back shop,
and the kettle will soon boil.' They found the
stock more than right; and I felt much obliged
to my million for its having enabled me to please
a worthy couple. I had occasion to be away for
half a year. When I came back I paid the corner shop a visit. My carpenter was boozing behind a quart pot, in the kitchen, in company with
a county court bailiff. The wife I had heard
scolding across the street. 'Curse you and your
shop,' growled the man at me. 'Why did you
give us anything — we never asked you — if you
were not going to keep it up?' The whole crew
is now in St. Giles and St. George's work-house."

I managed better with Cocksey and his wife, of Tripe Alley. Cocksey is a brewer's drayman, professionally inclined to liquor, and not fond of hard work. Mrs. Cocksey, with allowances for a woman's impediments in the pursuit of this sort of ideal, was not unlike him. They were a disreputable pair to be quartered on a locality which holds its head so deservedly high as Tripe Alley. Cocksey had good wages, but he and his wife were always out at elbows. Half their belongings were habitually in pawn. They were often without bread, which mattered more to Mrs. Cocksey than to Cocksey, for he had beer. I might have relieved them, for the sake of the Alley. But I was sure that, if I touched them with my little finger, I should have the pair on my hands, and for ever.

" Fortunately, as I was passing one morning, I remarked a flower box in their window. They were guiltless of it. A former tenant had left it behind. Never had I seen Cocksey with a flower in his coat, or his horses on May day itself decorated with oak leaves at their collars. I stepped into Carter's, and asked for the best auricula seeds. It was February, and I bought an assortment of the newest and rarest. With them I called on Mrs. Allen, the landlord's agent; that is, mine. She was a woman who could keep a secret; as she proved by not having let out whose property was the Alley, or good-bye to my rents. Mrs. Cocksey, as well as Cocksey, was, she said, out for the morning. She had a key to their room, and we went up together. I planted the seeds carefully, having first dressed the mould in the box with a patent fertilizer. I instructed Mrs. Allen how she was to do the watering, giving her a clothes-brush for it. One morning in April Cocksey was staring out of the window. 'What's this rubbish?' he called out, as he caught sight of green leaves peering above the mould. His wife looked. 'That's soon put right,' said she, and she was stretching out to pull up the stalks, when Cocksey savagely interposed: 'They don't harm you, and, as you didn't plant them, you've no call to meddle.' 'We shall have you going in for the flower show soon, and blue ribbons,' retorted she sarcastically. But she was too lazy to exert herself further. Both of them were, however, puzzled at the apparition, though they accounted for it by the eccentricity of some former inhabitant, or unconscious cerebration on the part of the box. First one, then the other, would, as by accident, approach the window, and stare. I have detected them at it from the outside myself.

"One brilliant Sunday morning in May I chanced

to be going up the staircase, and passed their open door. I heard a noisy exclamation, and I took the liberty to walk in. Husband and wife were by the open window, open-mouthed, and looking half in awe. An auricula had just burst into dusty glory. They scrutinized the box, and discovered dozens on the eve of beginning to bloom too. They were struck with wonder and delight, such as Adam may be supposed to have felt at the first sight of a peach tree in blossom.

"With the admiration awoke a sense of responsibility. They had not the least suspicion that Mrs. Allen had been tending the plants. About the early shoots they had not troubled their consciences. They had imagined those grew as the grass grows. With a resplendent flower it was different. They understood that needed to be nurtured. I was the Miriam to the Moses in the bulrushes. By my advice Mrs. Cocksey fetched up Mrs. Allen. She did not spare them. Mingling her instructed enthusiasm with their amazement, she made them feel that the possession of an auricula is a solemn trust, and she loaded them with pages learnt by heart out of Loudon. She called in neighbours, devoted to auricula-fancying, to admire. Among them they laid out several months' labour, in manuring, watering, transplanting, and

potting, to the end of October, for the Cocksey
household.   After a while the pair began to study
for themselves.   They grew learned in flowers, and
bartered, and exhibited.   Life had a new object.
They were up early and late, and eat the bread of
happy care.   Auricula-keeping reacted on Cocksey's
team, and his wages were raised.   As for her, when,
a few Saturdays ago, I met husband and wife at a
window-garden function, I found the slattern of
Tripe Alley as neat and well dressed as the best
of the company.   'Curious, wasn't it, Sir,' said
Cocksey, with a complacent smile ; ' there was that
poor soul Wilkins, must have shaken a bag with
some seeds at the bottom of it over the window
box ; and he never had the sense to know what
they were.   But they came up for me.   The difference between eyes and no eyes, is it not, Sir?'
' Very like,' said I.

"But I succeeded, I flatter myself, almost better
with Styles, the chairmender.   A drunken brute, if
ever there was one, was Styles.   Not a bad work-
man ; and then, after sitting out in rain, sun, and
frost all day, he would go home, drink the most of
a bottle of gin in his pig-sty of a room, beat his
wife and little boy, Dick, and sprawl in a tipsy
doze across the truckle-bed.   He never conversed
and never read.   Learning and scollards he sincerely hated.

"I thought and thought, till I had concocted a little plot. I picked up in Wellington Street 'Uncle Tom's Cabin,' first English edition, in original crumpled leaves, £20. I paid the coal and greengrocery woman to throw it in the coal basket when the boy came next to the shop. 'There's some paper,' she said, 'rubbish — I don't want it — to light your fire with.' The boy had just learnt to read, and then been taken away from school. No Board visitor had yet found him out. He pocketed the book, and, as soon as he was at home, drew it forth. He sat by the lamp, as his mother sewed button-holes. As he was not very proficient, he had to spell, and read out many sentences. His mother caught a few lines. 'Could you not read a little louder?' she asked. The boy read aloud in his shrill voice. They did not heed the man, who sat drinking by the table in the half-shade. Next day, when Dick looked for the book, it was gone, to his sorrow. He was afraid to question his father, who, he concluded, had tossed it into the fire.

"In the evening, rather earlier than usual, Styles came home. At once he went to the cupboard where he kept locked up his pipe and bottle. Something lay in his way at the bottom, and he kicked it out. It was 'Uncle Tom.' 'More rubbish,' he said. Dick stealthily caught it up, and, as soon as his father was safe at his pipe and gin, resumed his reading. The mother sewed and listened; the father smoked and drank, — a little while, — then leant his head on his arms on the table, and went off in a doze. He did not snore. In the morning he picked up the volume as he was starting for his work. He said: 'I know where they'll give me twopence for the trash.' Dick was too much scared to protest, and cried quietly. Away went father and 'Uncle Tom.' At night, to his wife's and son's surprise, both were back together. 'There's the thing; worth nothing,' he called roughly, yet almost sheepishly, to the boy, as he extracted it from his pocket. Dick was too well contented to comment, and seized the book as a jackal snaps at the broken meat from a lion's repast. Soon the reading began, and the listening, — two listenings. At last Styles stood up, put away his bottle, not his pipe, and crossed over, casually, to the fireplace. It had been raining hard, and he was wet to the bone. His clothes steamed. 'Damp-like,' said he, and sat down. Mrs. Styles told Dick to 'shut up.' 'Shut up yourself,' cried Styles, savagely. 'Can't you let the boy alone?' That night it was a late sitting. In the morning the man said as he went out: 'Dick, my lad, I

won't take the book away. But mind, you lazy
varmint, you're not to read till I be back. If you
do, I'll pack you off, without the book, to sell
matches.'

" 'Uncle Tom' was read through in course of
time. When it was done, I had mixed up 'Nicho-
las Nickleby' with the coals. More paraffin was
consumed in the family, and less gin. After
'Nickleby,' there was 'The Old Curiosity Shop';
then, 'Midshipman Easy,' and 'Masterman Ready.'
'Robinson Crusoe' followed; and now we are arrived as far as 'Ivanhoe.' All early editions,
remember, best impressions of the plates, thrown
in as waste firing with coals and cabbages. I
have never received a word of thanks. There
has never been the notion of a favour from
mortal man. But Styles brings home every
sixpence he earns; he has cut off his gin, and
taken to beer in moderation instead. Only in
moderation does he strap his son. He has not once
been to the Police Court since the readings opened,
for beating his wife. A few rough words do not
count. 'Rather wasted on Garden Court, Dickens
and Marryat first editions,' you think. I don't
know about that. At any rate, my chairmender
sticks to them, though he is grateful to nobody for
them. A neighbour heard Spykes, the second-hand

bookseller in Long Acre, bargaining for them. He offered other and well-bound copies in exchange, with thirty shillings to make all straight. 'You hain't a-going to have them,' said Styles. 'How do I know the words 'd be the same in those fine books of yourn?' Styles already has a valuable little library, without being in the least sensible that he owes, not it alone, but also his better food, clothes, and manners, a happier wife, a better-bred son, and an opened intelligence, to another than himself.

" Jenkins again ; Jenkins, the blear-eyed cobbler in Market Cut. Books were not what he needed. He has always been a greedy reader, and his reading turned sour on his temper. He led a wretched existence, and passed his misery on. His family and associates were all the worse for his bitter snarl. He never lost an opportunity of a sneer at me and my savings, though, to have anything put by, one could scarcely have less, I should think. I cudgelled my brains for the means of taming him, without enslaving his courageous spirit. He has twelve children, you should know, an imbecile wife, and a hump. Yet he has his own views on the Newfoundland, African, and Bulgarian questions, and very queer views they are.

" One afternoon I was passing his door, on my

way home to my chop, when I saw him hallooing in a fury. A cat flew by. 'Nasty vermin,' he said, 'be off!' I had my cue. Straight off I went to Ratcliff Highway. 'The handsomest Persian kitten,' I said, 'that you have. Price no object.' Though I dote on cats, I have never been able to afford myself a pure Persian. The shaggiest, cruellest little wretch ever beheld was brought out by the menagerie foreman. 'Do you want, Sir, a prize-winner?' he asked. 'If so, I will warrant this little brute hard to beat.' I paid the £25, and little enough for the beauty. The foreman wished to feed it before we left. 'By no means,' said I; 'I particularly want it hungry.' It was placed in a basket, and back I journeyed as sharpset as it to the Cut.

"The November evening was chill and black. The door of the buildings in which Jenkins sulked was shut. I rang his bell, took the kitten out of the basket, and slid round the corner. Down came Jenkins, and opened the door. 'Drat the boys!' said he, as nobody appeared. At that instant he became aware that something was rubbing at his legs. He looked. It was poor famished Kitty. 'Out!' he cried, when he saw that it was a cat. He gave it a push; but Kitty was hungry; and man, even with cross words and

feet, to a hungry kitten means milk.   It rubbed
on, soft, purry, furry, electrically fuzzy.   Jenkins
blinked a little more closely, and this time his push
was less decided.   Kitty understood, and arched
her back, and rubbed. 'You poor, little, ugly
beast,' said Jenkins.   'Just the way of the world.
Turned you out, did they, when they saw you were
plain and worthless?   Dare say it was Tibbs; like
Tibbs.   Pretends to like cats, does he?   And here
he is; kicks out the poor, miserable nigger, for
not being a fine tabby, like Madam who came
poaching at my swallows this afternoon.   All's
one; this ain't no Cats' Home, this ain't.   Get
out!   Can't be catching rheumatiz talking to you
all night.   Off with you!'   Oratorical denuncia-
tions of neighbours, though they are not milk, may
foreshadow milk, and Kitty had been purring and
rubbing in hope.   But it was over now; the vision
of a warm chimney-corner and a full saucer was
rudely shattered.   She understood the personal
peroration much too clearly.   All of a sudden she
poured her whole infantile soul into a mew.   It was
a mew like the cry Jenkins had uttered sixty-five
years before — a pinched, deformed baby foundling
— as the snowflakes began to follow him up the
Bermondsey Workhouse doorstep.   He stooped,
and felt the hollow sides, and looked into the exag-

gerated eyes. All Kitty's most thoroughbred Persian points were to him evidence of ill usage and stinted fare. 'I do believe they have driven you out without a sup,' said he. 'In with you,' he called roughly, and in he gently carried her, slamming the door, so that I heard no more.

"Next day I called. The youngest girl was at home, with her bedridden mother, nursing Kitty. 'A kitten!' I exclaimed. 'I never thought your father would let you keep a kitten.' 'No more did we,' was Susie's answer; 'but the little brute, as father calls it, — and it is rather ugly, the dear, — had been sent adrift, he thinks, by Mr. Tibbs, and was so hungry that father brought it into supper. This morning he said it might stay till over dinner. Here is father.' In walked Jenkins, and gave me a gruff good-day, a shade less gruff than usual. 'Nothing to do, poor gentleman, as in general,' said he. 'Like my wife there; but 'tain't her fault, after all, poor soul. I don't suppose you have had twelve children? I just came,' he proceeded, 'for my awl. Ah! there's little Ugly!' he interjected, as he gave the kitten a clumsy stroking, which she did not in the least resent, though she hissed when I looked at her. Obviously, me she recollected as a cat-stealer and cat-deserter, and Jenkins as her preserver. 'My

awl not here,' said Jenkins; and he left with a
lingering last look at Kitty. Kitty was not turned
out after dinner, or the next day, or the next day.
Ten days later I walked by the cobbler's stall,
and there was Mistress Kitty in attendance. She
grew and throve. 'Ugly, but good as gold,' was
Jenkins's estimate of her. If a cat-fancier ever
praised her looks, he treated it as sarcasm, and
replied in kind. He never seemed to suspect that
he was fortunate in the ownership of a priceless,
pure-bred Teherance, though he has been heard to
mutter, 'I half think, Kitty, I am getting to like
even the looks of you.'

"I am a little afraid that Kitty has cost Cogers'
Hall an orator, and Tom Paine a disciple. But
Mrs. and the Misses and Masters Jenkins have
more than proportionately benefited by an extraordinary and delightful abatement in the vivac-
ity of their indefatigable bread-winner's temper.
Not that the old Adam is incapable of revival.
You should have seen him when Potts, the rich
sporting publican, came to offer, first, £5, then
£10, and, by degrees, £30 for Kitty, now a grave
and portentously shaggy matron. Jenkins at
length lost his equanimity at the pertinacity of
his tempter, who saw his money back twice
over in prizes. 'Not if you were to make it

£50, and throw yourself in for cat's meat,' he passionately ejaculated, as he caressed his treasure with clinging hands and jealous eyes.

"It is not only costermongers and suchlike," pursued Mr. Griggs, "whom I have patronized without pauperizing. I presented a Hundred-Guilder Rembrandt to Bisque, who had done nothing but hoard, and would have done nothing else to the end of the chapter. A pretty penny it cost me; only, happily for him, it cost him fifty times as much. Grateful to me for it? Not a bit. But a connoisseur questioned it, and he went so deeply into its history to defend his property, that he ended by believing he had created its value. He perceived the necessity of bestowing worthy companions upon it, and indulged the wholesome vice of collecting. Perhaps you have read — I have not — his monograph on the Master's reason for blurring the Ass in the second state of the Flight into Egypt. At present there is not a madder collector in London than he; and I do not suppose that he puts by more than £20,000 a year.

"Then there is Smith-Rivers, a very good fellow, and a rising pedigree lawyer. Nobody can say that either the bounty of his maiden aunts, or mine, has injured him. His aunt Jemima, when she was dying, sent to consult me on her will.

'Shall I,' she asked, 'leave the boy £2000, or the family portraits?' 'The portraits, by all means,' was my reply. He was inclined to be lazy, and I knew an unearnt £2000 would set him longing for other treasure trove of the same description. He had eleven other maiden aunts, Smiths or Riverses, each with a thousand or two to bequeath, and a share of the two family portrait-galleries. The deceased was the acknowledged doyenne of the double sisterhood. The eleven other wills, it was understood, would be repetitions of hers. Smith-Rivers had always jeered quietly at the portraits. The legacy of an instalment of them killed the hope of money bequests, and raised the expectation of the complete family picture-gallery. He felt himself the head of the allied houses and restorer of their original grandeur. He dived into the abysses of heraldic and genealogical lore; and he has now no equal in scenting out a superannuated peerage claim. But I was conscious I was something in his debt for my advice. So I picked up a pair of undoubted Sir Joshuas, a Smith, — a namesake, at any rate, — and a Rivers. I sent the two as a New Year's gift to him at the cost of £2000.

"People talk of white elephants. A white elephant is a far more innoxious possession than an unearned sirloin of beef. A white elephant as a present may be a nuisance; it does not murder independence and the spirit of self-help. Give the objects of your beneficence, my dear young friend, be they destitute or not, something they never anticipated and never coveted. They will not be obliged at the time. They will not be savage with you hereafter. If you have chosen gifts to suit a vein in their characters not yet worked, and worth working, they may even be gainers as much as yourself by your palming off upon them some of your incumbrance. In any case, be careful to wrap your favours so carefully up that they will never be recognized as such. So long as one observes these precautions one may amuse oneself with charity, and hurt nobody in particular. Pray, how am I, who never have had a Thank you for a penny of the half-million I have given away, worse than Stiggins, who buys everything he uses of sweaters, for fear, he says, of demoralizing honest labour? However, it is all a matter of taste; and my taste is my taste, and Stiggins's is Stiggins's."

CHAPTER VII.

THE LAW-REVISER.

I WAS calling this morning — December 1 — on my lawyer — my temporary lawyer. He had sent me a demand for payment of a small account for boots. Some people might call him my boot-maker's lawyer. So he is; and mine, too. My habit in these cases is to adopt the other side's legal advisers, and treat the affair as if they were acting simply for me. It makes the tone of business more amiable. As I talked with a junior clerk, and suggested various methods of meeting the little difficulty without resort to the common-place cash method, I noticed an elderly gentleman sitting in a corner of the room, and listening. He went out before my interview was over. As I left, I found him in the outer office, speaking to a creepy creature, of the bailiff order, and examining bills of costs.

I was still at the bottom of the staircase, pondering my next financial move, when down walked the stranger. The stairs were worn, with abrupt turns, and he slipt heavily close by me. I stretched out my hand involuntarily, and saved him from a nasty fall. As it was, he had jarred himself, and I offered my arm. He accepted the courtesy, excusing himself for the trouble he gave by the explanation that he was in haste to cross Holborn to the Law Courts. As we walked, he talked. "I was listening," he said, " to your discussion in the office. Bills is a man of his word, and, I can see, means action. You had better raise something on your watch, and settle, to save costs." I thanked my companion for his gratuitous counsel, and told him that I was myself acquainted with a pawnbroker. I suspected that his purpose was to introduce me to his own, and pocket commission. "Happy to be of use," said he; "but come along, come along."

Though I had no reason for going with him, I had no real business anywhere else, and I scented a possibility of lunch. He took me into Mr. Justice Starkey's Court, where the suit of Spokes v. Stokes was then on. Robins, the alimentary liquorice man, died last year, leaving a will and codicil. He had quarrelled with Spokes, his only sister's husband, now dead, and had been heard to say that Spokes should have none of his money. Since then he had seen so little of the Spokeses, that it could not be proved he knew Spokes was dead, or where his sister, the widow, lived. Mrs. Stokes is godchild of an aunt of the testator. The Stokeses lived in Arundel-street, near him, and there was evidence that he had met Mr. Stokes twice at a vestry meeting, and nodded to him, or somebody else, once from an omnibus knifeboard. Just before he died, Mrs. Spokes, with her family of orphans, moved into Arundel Place, at the bottom of Arundel-street. When his will was read, it appeared that by it he had left £10 a year to his sister, Mrs. Spokes, and constituted the Cat Hospital at Brownlow Heath the residuary legatee. By a codicil he himself drew up after Mrs. Spokes had come a widow to Arundel Place, he revoked the will, appointed the *Spokes* family in Arundel-street his residuary legatees, in place of the Cat Hospital. Mrs. Spokes claimed the residue on the ground that Arundel-street was plainly a mistake for Arundel Place, where he might have discovered from the Post Office Directory that she lived; and that in the name of the family the down-stroke of the p manifestly deserved to be regarded instead of the cross-stroke of the t. As we entered the Court, his Lordship, who had finished hemming and hawing, and clearing his throat, was proceeding to deliver judgment. It was not very elabo-

rate.   His opinion was that he could not go outside the four corners of the will.   The testator
had an Englishman's right to prefer friendship to
family affection.   He had specified Arundel-street,
where his friends lived, and not Arundel Place,
where his sister resided.   He had deliberately crossed
his *t* to signify Stokes, and by accident let his pen
slip below the line, without intending to denote
Spokes.   Consequently, the residue must go to the
Stokeses, and not even the £10 a year to Mrs.
Spokes.

"I knew it all along," groaned my neighbour.
"What a scoundrelly thing is law !   But it shan't
have it its own way this time ; it shan't be let rob
widows and orphans, while Jack Button has his
million."   He took hold of my arm again, as if he
had a right to it, so corroborating a recent suspicion of mine that I had lighted on another millionaire.   The Court was adjourning for luncheon,
and we went out in the crowd of retiring clients,
solicitors, and counsel.   Mr. Button — as I gathered
was his name — hobbled up to a little downcast
group, — a faded, middle-aged lady, with three
pleasant-looking daughters, who were telling her
not to mind.   A gentleman with a solicitor's bag
was standing by their side.   Mr. Button seemed
to know him.   "Here's the deed," said Mr. But-

ton. "At least, it will be bread and cheese. I was sure your precious Courts could not do an honest thing. So I had it stamped at Somerset-house yesterday, on the chance." While he talked, the solicitor had been glancing over the document. When he had done, he turned to Mrs. Spokes and her daughters. "Really, ladies," he said, "Mr. Button has put the Court again right. Law has deprived you of £17,650, and by this conveyance the exact sum is made over to you and my charming young friends." The poor woman did not understand. When Mr. Button's little piece of amiable spite upon justice was explained to her, she at once, with many thanks, began to decline the gift. "That is a pity," said Mr. Button; "for, if you won't have it, Stokes takes. Read the deed yourself. Either Spokes or Stokes, just as in that precious codicil." The lawyer confirmed the assertion; and good Mrs. Spokes, who had no idea of doubling the windfall of the Stokeses, saw she had no alternative.

"Come along," cried Mr. Button to me; "it is time for my chop, and I have business after." Here was a money-bag with a leak in it, through which a score of thousands trickled off-hand. I love to be with money, — sacks of money, — and Mr. Button was still lame enough to be glad of my arm. Naturally we went to the Cock, where he ordered a chop and follow for each of us. As we waited, I thought I had better make certain that I was not wasting my day. I asked him outright if he were a millionaire. "Why not?" he returned. "Well," I said, "everybody is not a millionaire, I presume." "Most people that I am acquainted with are," he said. "Are not you?" "Most certainly," I remarked sarcastically, "or I should not be in trouble about boots." Without taking the hint he said: "Oh, that shows nothing. There is not a man in my set who has not a county court summons issued against him pretty well every week. Why, Plutus Harris has just done seven days for what they term contempt of court."

I returned to the incident of the morning, which he treated as a trifle. But the topic led to others, and I gathered an idea, gradually, of his present vocation in life. "My business," he said, "is to put the law courts right. They know I am on their track, and they don't like it. I foil their knavish tricks continually. Only last week I was before the Lords Justices. That is, the Duchess of Netherby was, and I was acquainted with her sad case. The late Duke left her without a farthing beyond her pitiful settlement of £3000 a year. She tried to upset the will, and failed. Their Lordships declared she had not a leg to stand on. I do not remember if those were their precise words. But I was to the fore. Off I went to my lawyer, and before night had conveyed to her the keep of a brougham and pair, and a house at Brighton.

"One of the follies of law is to affect to be infallible; so it is obliged to choose between two claimants, and assign the whole to one when there is not a pin's head of difference in their rights. Now I have retained half a dozen first-rate counsel. They are too judicial ever to have held a brief, unless by pure accident. For the same reason they will never rise to the bench; and they have all their lives been reading law and meditating on justice. Out of them I constitute courts of appeal. Many is the judgment we have reversed, with costs.

"I can give you instances in plenty of the need for my tribunal. Last week I dropped into the Queen's Bench Division. The Judges were deciding one of their favourite questions — a contention between two innocent victims of a fraudulent attorney. The counsel on both sides were acquaintances of mine, and I borrowed the papers as the argument proceeded. Plaintiff and defend-

ant were equally to be pitied, and one would have
to bear the whole loss. The moral balance was
exactly even. One was an aged, kind-hearted
widow; the other, a graceful orphan girl. The
girl had the superior equitable title; the widow
had the first legal interest. I leant over to the two
juniors, and asked, 'Which will win?' 'A toss-
up,' they whispered back. I beckoned to the solicitors in the well to come to me outside. 'Now,' I
said, 'if your clients be sensible women, and will
share, I am ready to pay all the heavy costs of this
folly.' They had some compassion for the poor
creatures, and agreed. During the luncheon recess
all concerned conferred. The result was that
when the court resumed, the leader for the plaintiff rose, and said the case was settled. What a
temper the Judge was in! He had been wasting
the whole luncheon half-hour in looking up the
authorities to deliver a learned impromptu judgment.

"Ten days ago I positively heard, with my own
ears, old Mr. Justice Sole say sonorously, as he decided a case: 'A cruel litigation this, Mr. Jobson;
it should never have come into court'; upon which
he decided against the side he was commiserating.
That, too, was a widow's case. There being no
settlement, her husband had, with a placid con-

science, put a small fortune which had come to her — that is, to him — after marriage, into the settlement of a daughter by a former marriage. Then he had died, leaving its rightful owner a pauper. What was I to do? What else could you, or any honest-feeling man of means, have done? Of course, I had to replace out of my own pocket the property which an iniquitous system of logical and scientific jurisprudence had stolen.

"Then there is the appeal nuisance and persecution. A plaintiff or defendant wins before a Judge sitting alone, before a divisional Court, and before the Court of Appeal. His opponent goes doggedly on to the House of Lords, where the tables are turned. The original conqueror has to pay all the costs incurred through a troop of Judges not apprehending the law. That is, he would have, if I had not made my million. As I have, and as the State will not take the consequences of the blunders of its own legal machinery, I must.

"Yes; it is expensive, and tantalizing too, having to stand by and see combatants batter one another about, when one knows oneself will have to bear the charges of the entire quarrel. But it is very seldom possible to step in before the end, and get ahead of the law, though I did it

once delightfully.   You remember the great Loch-
even suit, do you not?   One of the common Scotch
kind.   Thirty thousand a year for one or other of
the two claimants who could prove that his ances-
tress had been made an honest woman by her
good man before his death.   'Thirty thousand a
year, or beggary,' said my informant.   'There's
an issue for you, and all dependent on the word
of a drunken cobbler, who heard, or thought he
heard, his chum, tipsy Rob Messop, call the woman
" that devil of a goodwoman of mine."'   'Do you
mean,' I asked, 'that one will have all, and the
other nothing?'   'Certainly; nothing,' was the
answer.

"I managed to be introduced to each, and invited them to dine.   They were in humble circumstances, and I gave them such a dinner as
they had never had before.   When they were very
comfortable, and also particularly friendly together,
I remarked that by that day week one would be
in a position to fare in the same way continually,
and the other might starve on a dunghill.   'What
a pair of idiots you are,' I said, 'to take the risk.
Why not agree that the loser shall have Happuck,
which is worth a clear £5000 a year?   Is not the
other £25,000 a year enough for the winner?'
You will hardly believe me, but they had never

seen it in that light. They slept on the idea.
In the morning they instructed their lawyers to
draw up a joint deed to the effect. The hearing
came on, and the drunken cobbler was believed.
Last autumn I was staying at Happuck, and the
laird asked over his big neighbour to meet me.
Both were exceedingly obliged to me, particularly
Happuck.

"Have you ever tacked a mortgage, by the
by?" he asked me. I said no, and inquired if it
were of the lock-stitch sort. "Well," he said, "I
was as blissfully ignorant as you of the atrocious
piece of casuistry till I happened to be before that
very acute and short-tempered Equity Judge, Sir
A. White. As soon as I entered the Court I could
perceive that something was up. His Lordship
and Crappit, the eminent conveyancer, who hate
one another, and are generally as mutually churl-
ish and snappish as two church beadles, were ami-
cable and almost jovial. Knowing that this boded
ill to litigants, I asked the usher the reason. All
the officers know me. 'Oh,' he said, 'they are
tacking mortgages.' I made a reporter explain the
horrid trickery. A man lends £100 on an estate
worth £30,000. Next, another man — that is,
another man's solicitor — lends £10,000 upon it.
Lastly, a money-lender, who has already sucked

the spendthrift owner dry, accepts the land as
security for a desperate £40,000. He goes to the
lender of the £100, and buys his first mortgage.
Thereupon he himself becomes first mortgagee.
That enables him to tack, as they term it in their
jargon, his third mortgage on the first, squeezing
out altogether the poor bodkin of a £10,000. Did
you ever hear of anything so ingeniously iniquitous? That was what was refreshing the black-
letter souls of Mr. Justice White and Mr. Jonadab
Crappit. Both were stone-deaf; but they could
hear their own brutal jokes, which they cracked,
as thick as thieves, while they pretended to pity
the poor ousted second mortgagee. I did better.
I took a transfer of the second mortgage, paying
the full price; and the whole black-letter gang
had the disappointment to find they were mangling me, who did not care a brass farthing for
the £10,000, instead of the victim they had fancied they were worrying.

"Law is always playing ill-tempered practical
jokes, like this tacking puzzle; and, so far as one
million can, I manage to foil its manœuvres. Did
you hear how I turned the laugh against Mr. Justice Snigges? He is one of those who, just like
old Sole, and old White, are constantly grieving
over the necessity of depriving honest men of

their own, and, on profound juridical principles,
are constantly doing it. Last Hilary sittings I
heard him myself avowing that it must appear
contrary to natural justice, equity, and reason, to
give judgment against one of the two parties, a
foreigner; and he immediately proceeded to give
it. The man was robbed, the Judge acknowledged,
of £200, and it would have been the same, he
added, if the sum at stake had been £200,000.
The wrong his Lordship imputed wholly to the
operation of a technical rule, which, in the re-
coded opinion of one learned Lord, had, if it ever
were law, been cancelled by the Judicature Act.

"I was boiling over with fury, which was but
half allayed by my despatch of a cheque for
the amount, with costs, to Bordeaux, when, by
good luck, I ran against Sykes of Brass Inn.
I expressed my indignation to him. 'You are
avenged,' he said; 'poor old Snigges, who is fond
of his money, has been himself caught in the
legal meshes.' I asked for an explanation. It
appeared that his Lordship was trustee for a Mr.
and Mrs. Wood, who had inherited shares in the
Cairngorm Bank. It is a limited bank, but with
a considerable amount of the capital not called up.
The shares could not be sold, under Mrs. Wood's
father's will, without the assent of Mrs. Wood,

which she refused to the Judge, unless she could
get a high premium. She preferred the bank's
eight per cent to three and a quarter from railway debentures. Sir T. Snigges had frequently
requested leave to sell the shares at any price,
and always in vain, till last March, when they
became unsaleable. The bank broke, and the
liquidator put the Judge on the list. There
was no other trust property, and Mr. Wood,
though rich, treated as a jest an invitation from
the Judge's solicitor to regard the liability as his.
'It was bad enough,' he said, 'to lose his wife's
£500 a year.'

"'After all,' continued Sykes, 'your revenge is
not very complete, for Snigges is rolling in money.
The £4000 he is out of pocket won't matter to
him.' 'What difference?' I cried, 'can it make
whether he be rich or ill off? The injustice is
the same, that he should have to pay instead of
the Woods. Is there really no way of putting the
thing straight?' 'None,' said Sykes, 'of forcing
Wood to bear his own proper burden. But there
are the shares at Pratt's office in Plumbago Buildings. Snigges is a nasty fellow to have to bring
to book. I dare say,' he added sarcastically, 'the
liquidator would not object if you bought them
even at this late date from the Judge's broker,

who has had them the last six months for sale!'
I hailed a Hansom, and drove to Plumbago Buildings. 'Have you not,' I inquired, 'forty Cairngorm shares for sale?' 'Yes, at 3% above par,'
was the answer; 'but, you know, the bank is
burst up.' 'The very reason,' I said, 'why I
want them. I am looking to a realization of the
assets. Hand the certificates over. Dobbs, with
whom I have had many dealings, looked at me
to see I was not joking. He perceived I was
serious, and had the sale note made out without
more ado. 'I understand,' he said; 'you are
going to prosecute the directors. What a Quixote
you have grown!'

"I went direct to the liquidator's office with the
certificate and sale note. Before he had recovered
from his surprise, I sat down and wrote a cheque
for £4000. 'Very singular, all this,' said the
liquidator. 'You know shares cannot pass now.
Still, £4000 is £4000, and it might be a twelvemonth before I screwed it out of his Lordship.
So here goes.' He gave me a formal receipt in
full discharge of the unpaid calls; and the peremptory demand he had just prepared for trans-
mission to the Judge was never sent. When
Snigges, who had been wondering at this delay,
heard the story, he was as cross as two sticks.

But he could not pick a hole in the transaction. The shares had been duly passed to me by his own broker. If he tried to upset the sale, I was, as he had cause to know, as obstinate as he, and would have fought him up and down the Courts for the rest of his life. After all, too, it was only tit for tat for his ridiculous judgment in Maistre *v.* Wiggins.

" I do little," continued Mr. Button, " in criminal law. But now and then it occurs to me to saunter into the Old Bailey. Some time since I was there, while a servant-girl was being tried for stealing. Her brother, it appeared, kept a small shop in Camden Town, which did not answer very well. His wife had just been brought to bed of twins, and an elder child had ricked her back dangerously by falling downstairs. On the top of these disasters came a distress levied by the landlord. The sister was housemaid in a charming house near London, surrounded by pleasant grounds, which I had often admired. The brother, to whom she was tenderly attached, sent her word of his sad plight. The next day was Sunday, — her Sunday out, — and she set off with her little store of savings to help him.

" As she left her master's gate, just inside, she saw a £5 note lying on the ground. Of course, she should have taken it to the house, and might have, if there had been more than the barest number of minutes to catch the only Sunday afternoon train. As it was, she picked it up, and reached her brother's. He and his were in a state of shabby and despairing misery, all for the want of £7 10, which, between her own money and the windfall, she had in her pocket. The temptation to be an angel from heaven was too great. She told herself, and her brother did not dissent, that it was a stray to which she and he had as good a title as anybody. She gave him the whole, and ran off in a glow of illegitimate delight.

"On her return at ten o'clock, she was met by the village policeman at the railway station, and led off to the lock-up. Her master had dropped a bank-note, which was loose in his pocket, as he pulled out his handkerchief, and a stable-boy had seen the girl stoop ten minutes afterwards, and run in a hurry down the road. The evidence was complete, and it never occurred to her to deny the facts, only the intention. She was convicted, and I by chance assisted at the trial. A juvenile barrister, ignorant and brazen, whom the Court asked to defend her, addressed a futile appeal, out of King Lear, to the compassion of the prosecutor, who, having amassed a fortune out of groceries,

thought an example ought to be made. The
Judge, not a real judge, reminded the prisoner
and the jury that charity should be practised with
one's own, and not with other people's money.
The upshot was a short term of imprisonment,
with a blasted character and broken heart thrown
in.

"For her I did what I could; what was it all?
But in another direction I succeeded better. By a
curious coincidence I owned a bit of ground opposite to the employer's premises. I went straight
from the Central Criminal Court to the temporary
offices of a new Suburban Light Soil and Basket
Necropolis Company. It had its capital, its secretary, and every thing, except only a gravelly site.
My little property was the exact thing it desired.
I sold it a bargain — well, a bargain, I hope, for
both of us. Sir, in the course of a year, to the
other attractions of Mr. Elkanah Whistle's sumptuous villa was added the exciting spectacle of the
march past his garden gates, every day of an ordinarily unhealthy week, of a score of genteel funeral
cavalcades.

"Another day I was at Worship-street Police
Court — not on my own account. The magistrate
was discoursing to a dangerous ruffian, who stood
in the dock, handcuffed, between two policemen.

His Worship was informing Jerry Swap that he was the terror of his neighbourhood. He had smashed the face of a good-looking girl with whom he lived past all recognition, and had kicked a couple of constables so savagely that their lives were in peril for a month. The magistrate wound up in tones almost awestruck that he could inflict no less a penalty than imprisonment for three months. 'What then?' I asked a woman at the back of the Court. 'Just this,' was the reply, 'that he will be at us the day he is loose, and it will be Hell in Eden Gardens.'

"'We'll see about that,' I said to myself. I went to the man who supplies me with my chuckers-out. For a small fee I had already procured from a policeman precise particulars of the size, weight, habits, and fighting ways of the local tyrant. I gave them to my purveyor with orders for a match, with something over, in those respects. He had the required article in stock, and fetched it forthwith. It — that is, Jem Buss — is a tremendous bruiser, with a nose as flat as the palm of my hand, and no forehead to speak of, yet, withal, as mild as a calf. I gave him three months' holiday, with instructions where to report himself after it. He kept his appointment to the minute, affable and happy, at the gates of the Middlesex

Model Lodging-house. Jerry was being discharged
at the moment, and I showed him to Jem.   I
explained to Jem that his business was to wait on
Jerry till Jerry should be quite satisfied. After
two months Jerry was like a lamb—not a Notting-
ham lamb.   I told Jem to bring him to a free-and-
easy tea and shrimps, and I never saw a prettier-
behaved fellow.   That is the real homœopathic
regimen — in large globules — for the rescue of a
district from human pests."

He beckoned the waiter, reckoned up the items,
and paid, with twopence for attendance.   I had to
make a return for his hospitality, and I said a few
words of admiration for his conscientiousness.   I
was no hero-worshipper, I protested; but benevolence like his stirred me to enthusiasm.   "I don't
know," he said, "about conscientiousness and
benevolence.   That's the sort of stuff Partridge
—Tobias Partridge of Highbury Pavement—
talks.   What I know, Sir, is, I hate your stuck-up
Perfection of Reason, which is perpetually acting
like a stark, staring fool! My business in life is
to circumvent her ignorant pranks!"   And he
shook his fist at large in the direction of the Law
Courts, or the Griffin.

CHAPTER VIII.

FORTUNE'S REDRESSER.

I AM too well bred to question or contradict a millionaire, and I let Mr. Button indulge as much as he liked in his tirades against infallible English Justice. But I remembered I had heard of certain passages in his early career, when he was in training for a millionaire, which might in some degree explain his irascibility. Of the ground for his incidental outburst against Mr. Tobias Partridge, I meant to judge for myself. My invariable method is to use one millionaire as a stepping-stone to another. They all hang together. By passing oneself judiciously on through the various members of the class it is astonishing what a large acquaintance it is possible in a moderate period to accumulate among them. Thus Mr. John Button's transient allusion fell upon fruitful soil. I did not heed the implied sneer; for I have discovered that it is impossible for one millionaire to speak the truth of another millionaire. It was enough for me to have unimpeachable testimony to the bona fides of the million. Millionaires, at

all events, have an unerring touch for their kind.
Here, moreover, was a millionaire of a species I
had heard of, but had never yet come in contact
with, — the owner at once of a million and a conscience.

Though Highbury Pavement is scarcely on my
beat, I determined that I would lose no time
in inspecting the phenomenon. All self-respecting houses on the Pavement — and none are
not self-respecting — come out in spring in a
blaze of hyacinths. That occupied by Mr. Partridge was as gay as its neighbours, and surprised
me generally by its neatness. Neatness, whether
in house fronts or in shirt fronts, is not an ordinary attribute of millionaires, who can well afford
to be untidy. I rang, and a second amazing incident was that I was immediately admitted. There
was not even the terrier which many of them keep
to probe the texture of a visitor's trousers with its
teeth.

I began to be a little afraid that Mr. Button
himself might have been deceived on the extent of Mr. Partridge's means. But he speedily
bustled in, and I was fully reassured. By this
time I was become intimately familiar with the
millionaire physiology. One feature every millionaire, who is not one by mere accident, invariably

exhibits. Mr. Partridge showed it in perfection. It is a crease under the left eye, between the parietal nerve and the nose. Of course, I do not mean that a man must have a full million to grow it. This, however, I can say for certain, I have never observed it under less than half a million. In a note to the hundred and thirty-seventh edition of Mr. Darwin's work on the "Origin of Species" it is minutely described under the name of *ruga sestertiensis*. The single chance of a mistake in identifying millionaires by it is that, like similar features, it is transmitted. Consequently, as every millionaire has a prodigal heir, the wrinkle may line the countenance of a dissolute pauper. Of that I was willing to take my chance for the sake of a study of character so interesting as was reported to be Mr. Partridge's; and my faith was rewarded.

Mr. Partridge was as civil as his maid-servant, though less self-confident and more hurried. "Yes, my good Sir," he commenced, as if he had been a dentist; "where is the ache? Sit down, and tell me all about it." I had, somewhat reluctantly, to confess that I had no specific indictment to lodge against destiny. I had ventured, I said, to call in order to be edified by an account of his remarkable experiences. "Well," he sighed, "that's rather a pity; still, everything must have a beginning. I like hearing cases better than going into my own. But you are welcome, till you have grown a grievance against fortune, to any good you can derive from my rather commonplace story.

"I cannot be described as born of poor but honest parents. My paternal grandfather was an Army contractor, and my father held a patent office with nothing to do. Between them I inherited a competence. My maternal grandfather, a prosperous attorney, increased this by his will to a very handsome amount. As you may imagine, then, I was trained in the creed that whatever is is right. But there was a wild strain in me. Somewhere in the stock there had been a conscience. The germ had for generations never had a chance of fertilization till it came to me. For me its whole rebellious energy unluckily was reserved.

"I had been brought up to no particular business, except the management of my own property. I quickly manifested a wonderful aptitude for that. Millionaires, I have heard Boggis say, are made, not born. There are, he declares, born knaves, born poets, born fools, but no born millionaires. I believe I am an instance to the contrary. I am sure I never trained myself to be a millionaire. An instinct in me seemed to force me to shift and change investments, scarcely with any consciousness on my part of a reason for the choice. I shuffled in and out, carrying at each remove a lengthening golden chain. Every bubble I touched solidified, till I blew it away, when instantly it burst. I went into a Rotten Fish Phosphorus Company, and the shares leaped up to five hundred per cent. I sold, and the concern liquidated. I bought the freehold of a used-up suburban cemetery, which immediately the Mid West Junction Railway required for its central station at a price of fiftyfold my purchase money. I speculated in a tontine for the fee of three carcass terraces in a suburban wilderness. Within a year and a half all the nominee local market gardeners but my representative succumbed to an epidemic local ague, leaving me in occupation. In another year appeared Dr. Gilseng's monumental book on climate, which proved that Malarial Gardens combined all the essential hygienic conditions. There was a rush of speculators, builders, and Pompeian architects to the spot, and they insisted on buying me out at a thousand times the trifle I had given.

"I never understood why I and my money danced in and out, always with preposterous profits. A power in me, greater and more imperative than myself, dictated. Continually I felt more and more uncomfortable. I knew what I gained others must have lost, and appeared to myself like a receiver of stolen property. My conscience, which grew daily more and more objurgatory, I am bound to say, may not have been strictly logical. It did not torment me about my hereditary possessions, which, if all I have casually heard of my maternal and paternal grandsires be true, may have travelled to them through rather miry ways. At their date it had not awoke, and therefore seemed to think it was not compromised by their obliquities. For me it held itself answerable, and I had quadrupled their illicit gains.

"It was constantly at me, wagging, carping, stinging. I stood its very plain-spoken and contumacious criticisms, till I was some distance into my second million, when I resolved to halt. Perhaps I ought to have stopped before; but I had always made up my mind that, sooner or later, I would follow the example of a well-known publican, and restore fourfold. Now, with £50,000, or even £100,000, you cannot restore fourfold. The figures will not let you, if you are to retain a decent competence for yourself. With a real good armful of savings you can, at any rate, begin, with

a fair chance that you will not be pulled up sharp.
Yes, I could very likely have started at the half
million; but, in truth, a man hardly has the opportunity then of pausing. The ball is rolling too
fast. He finds himself at and past his million
before he perceives where he actually is.

"At all events, right or wrong, there I did
stand. At first, turned out in the open with a
million and a half in one heavy bundle on one
shoulder, and a conscience as heavy on the other,
I can tell you I felt pretty uncomfortable and
desolate. But I set to work at length, and I have
been working hard for the past dozen years. 'A
practical philanthropist,' you say. Nothing of the
kind. My business simply is restitution. It is
not my fault that I am absurdly rich, and it is not
other people's fault — I mean, some other people's
fault — that they are intolerably poor. Fortune
merely is in the habit of playing at hunt the
slipper with money. She snatches from one to
toss to another; and, obviously, the duty of the
other is to try to square matters. Every millionaire is, often innocently enough, a thief. Something does not come out of nothing. An honest
man ought to look about and trace the true owner.

"That is what I aim at. I do not pretend to
be able to label my thousands severally with the

names of the particular pockets from which they
have been abstracted. But I endeavour to classify
them; and I appropriate the proceeds of each sort
of pillage to the victims of analogous though not
necessarily identical frauds. In my own case it
would be ridiculous, I very speedily learnt, to
attempt to recoup the contributors to my million.
It would have only been to transfer the trouble
I take to another conscientious millionaire. My
sheep have all been such born idiots, that if their
fleeces were given back to them, they would insist
forthwith on being shorn again. From the time
I moved into Highbury from the Albany, where
the porter objected to having to explain the way
to my chambers to crowds of afflicted and peculiarly muddled applicants, my system has been to
search out intelligent and meritorious butts of Fortune in different categories, who would benefit
permanently by being put on propertied legs again.
I walk, metaphorically, the hospitals with a preference for the accident wards. I have no liking
for workhouse infirmaries, and asylums for incur-
ables or imbeciles.

" You would like to have some instances?
Well, you must not expect anything very sensa-
tional. I daresay you have heard of the great
Feversham bankruptcy. No man could have been

more honourable, ingenious, and industrious than
James Feversham. A great public benefactor, too,
for upwards of twenty years. His process for the
elimination of blacks — London blacks, not African
blacks — completely falsified the Registrar-General's
estimates of urban mortality. I can appreciate its
value, as I made £20,000 out of my holding in
a similar undertaking for the conversion of the
residuals into a medicinal ointment. However, I
was luckier than Feversham. The shares in my
company rose to a tremendous premium, when I
sold, and the concern burst up.

"No; I am not aware how much business it
ever did. Poor Feversham would have been more
fortunate if he had done as little. His system was
so prodigiously efficacious that, after he had made
a very fine property, he was induced to buy concessions for the establishment of his apparatus in
every large town in the kingdom. The whole of
his capital was embarked in the purchases and in
the consequent erections. Just at that moment
the present system for the absolute preliminary
purification of fuel came suddenly into operation.
There were no longer any blacks to be eliminated.
All the engines and buildings were thrown as
waste lumber upon Feversham's hands, with an
annual charge of £50,000 to the municipalities

for their concessions for the next ten years. The town councils would not abate a penny of their claims, and Feversham did not think of disputing his liability. He never was a very practical man in money matters. He gave up his million and everything, and the creditors, I believe, eventually received twenty shillings in the pound.

"They presented him with a most laudatory testimonial. The chief one showed me a copy. I asked after the family. 'Poor souls,' said my informer, 'what a change for them! From the lap of luxury, not that they were ever extravagant, to a lodging at Pentonville. Feversham earns £2 a week as a German correspondence clerk. He speaks and writes four languages, you know. The three daughters are visiting governesses.' 'Surely,' I remarked, 'their many friends should not allow this.' He shrugged his shoulders: 'The ups and downs of life!' said he, as he drove off to present the magnificent sheet of illuminated vellum. To my mind — in its existing stage, I mean — the thing was an atrocity. I would not suffer it. It was a disgrace to the millionaire profession, which I was resolved to clear away. With the help of my lawyer I manufactured a plausible deceased second cousin twice removed, and he bequeathed to a most deserving though unknown relative £20,000.

Finally, it cost me something extra. A clerk of my solicitor's unluckily was on the staff of a society paper. A paragraph appeared, of which Somerset House caught hold. It came down upon Messrs. Subway, of New Square, for probate duty, which I had to refund to them. However, a financial wrong had been practically corrected; and you will not find a pleasanter cottage than Mr. Feversham's on Leith Hill, or a more accomplished and contented household.

"Sometimes," recommenced Mr. Partridge, after showing me a set of remarkable paintings in an upstairs room, "the call for redress comes from another direction than that of commerce. Doubtless you are conversant with the mournful history of the artist whose works you are so good as to admire. I bought the pictures one gusty March afternoon in a Bond-street auction-room, because they took my fancy. There were no advances on my modest bids. Not a broker in the place had ever heard of Vincent Tremuse. Yet, as the auctioneer observed, every picture had been exhibited in the Royal Academy. The next May the whole art world was gazing in a rapture on two Dorsetshire idyls, a pair, by the same Tremuse. Before the season was over he had been elected an Associate of the Academy. Not that the honour was of

much pecuniary use; for he never touched brush
and palette more. He was dead before the autumn
ended. He died of a disease with a Greek name,
and I asked his doctor the meaning. 'The consequence of not having had enough to eat for the
past few years,' he said.

"I made a note of the fact, though I may say
for myself that I could do nothing for Tremuse.
Personally, I was not conscious of his market
value till the art critics suddenly awoke to it;
and the poor fellow had left no kinsfolk. I recollected him, however, when I was at Burlington
House last May, and saw a work of manifest
genius, as it appeared to me, skied. It seems I
was not mistaken in this instance. I asked Sir
James Edmundson his opinion. 'Yes, admirable,'
he replied; 'not that you are the first to discover
poor Maurice's merit. We all know he is brim-
ming over with cleverness; but he is an obstinate
fool, and will not go in for photography in oils.'

"I bought the painting, and ascertained the
artist's address. I found him working in a
wretched hole. Through the thin walls pene-
trated the cries of peevish, sickly children — his.
I looked round. The walls of the studio, or what
did duty for one, were covered with brilliant canvases. Others were stacked on the floor. After a

few questions, I went off to the Attic Art Society, and brought the secretary back in a cab. He was surprised and delighted. I guaranteed the expense of an exhibition of Mr. Maurice's works. It was held, and the critics, whose eyes were actually opened to them now for the first time, raved in their enthusiasm. Half were sold in the rooms, and the remainder I took at the same average price. I have no cause to repent of my bargain, though I did not seek for profit. Try to be allowed to give him a commission now, and you will be favoured if you have your picture delivered five years hence.

"The odd thing," he resumed, after a pause to take breath, "is when people clearly understand the pitiableness of a case, and have the power of relieving it, yet don't. Then it is that a millionaire with a conscience comes in handily. The combination is really at times much more convenient than you might suppose. Yesterday, for example, my friend Swaffham, Lord Swaffham, called here with a subscription list. A melancholy case, he explained. Raynes, a Warwickshire squire, and M. F. H., had made himself responsible for a patent brick compost company. In the usual way it failed. The creditors had come down upon him and sold him up, to the last stick. 'What!' I

exclaimed; 'Raynes, the man who gave to South
Kensington his grand-uncle's Boningtons, after
Dircks of Bond-street had offered him £60,000
for the set?' 'The same,' said he. 'In a terrible
state, I fear; a galloping consumption, his doctor
reports. We want to raise £300 to send him for
the winter to the South.'

"Now Swaffham is not merely a Viscount, but
a new, and therefore a solvent, Viscount. Every
new Viscount has to settle a clear £500,000 on
the title. 'A friend of yours?' I inquired. 'Like
a brother,' he said; 'you see, I have given £20.
If nine other men will give as much apiece, the
thing is done. I don't mind if I wear out a pair
of boots in beating up enough subscribers. I am
not going to let such a good fellow die for lack of
a little sunshine.' 'No, indeed,' I said; 'though
I have no right to say I am anything like a
brother.' So I took my pen, and wrote £280
under Swaffham's £20. He was effusive in his
thanks, as well he might be, for he had saved his
boots. He called my act heroic. I call it simple
justice — vicarious justice, though; justice ren-
dered to Raynes by Partridge *vice* Swaffham."

CHAPTER IX.

HERE we were interrupted by the maid-servant, who said Mr. Stuckham was at the door. Mr. Partridge ordered that he should be shown in, whispering to me: "A good-tempered man, but no principle, no sense of obligation." Mr. Stuckham, a little old winter-apple-faced gentleman, with the *ruga sestertiensis* very fairly developed, explained his call. He wanted to know whether Mr. Partridge meant to undertake the Brodderty case. Mr. Partridge answered that he had gone into it, and reluctantly had arrived at the conclusion that Mr. Hugh Brodderty's calamity was not one of fortune's tricks, and had been deliberately incurred by himself. Mr. Stuckham, therefore, was welcome to it.

Mr. Stuckham seemed relieved. "A blessing to me," he said, "that I have no mission. I can please myself." I did not conceal my curiosity — I never do — and Mr. Partridge introduced me to his visitor. Mr. Stuckham was kind enough to say that I had the sort of countenance which always interested him, the expectant face. "That's my weakness," he said, "which Partridge always laughs at; I cannot resist expectation. But it is just as well for our friendship. It keeps us from clashing. His objects hardly ever expect. When it is direct bad luck, not their own fault at all, down they go; and they stop down, as a rule, unless he be there to drag them up. Sometimes there is a case on the line like Brodderty's; not often. Generally it is Box and Cox with us. When people have not had a right to expect a disaster, then it is his turn. When they had no right to expect good, then it is mine.

"Mine's the more comfortable way, at all events. No fuss in tracing rights and wrongs; merely see that a man is disappointed and give him his appointment. Only this morning I watched a stupid vagabond running the whole length of Gower-street after a railway cab with a surly footman on the box by the driver. He might have known he was not wanted. I kept saying to myself as he ran: 'You'll be warned off; you'll be warned off.' Yet I heard him growl, as he was warned off, according to my prediction, 'All my luck!' So I gave him his sixpence. Then there was the blacking man's will last week, which I had to put right. The will cut off with a shilling his nephew Harry, who had married at his orders to keep up the family, and has a dozen children. All the young fool's fault for coming to his uncle's tea-party, two years back, in patent leathers instead of boots polished with Martindale. Thought Martindale had repented of his rather excessive severity. So he had, and was substituting the young one's name for the Clodhoppers' Home, when he died holding the pen with which he had meant to execute the codicil. Harry had no cause to be aggrieved; his own doing; but he was, and I carried out his uncle's real intention.

" Old Jervis's affair was something of the same sort, only a little more complicated. You recollect the Clan Tulloch Peerage case. Jervis never had the ghost of a chance, and went on petitioning and petitioning, and paying costs, for eight years. The Lords gave it finally and forever against him. It was not a peerage he wanted; had refused one over and over again. But he had set his heart on being Clan Tulloch. He was inconsolable, or appeared to be; and I pitied him greatly. What could I do? You can't buy a peerage, — at any rate, a Plantagenet one.

" Happily I remembered he was an egg-collector, and as happily that there was a single gap in his marvellous collection. For half his life, long before he heard of Clan Tulloch, he had been coveting an egg of the Painted Auk. Except at the British Museum, the Copenhagen Museum, and the Ashmolean, none was known to be in existence. His loss, at the Selborne sale, to the British Museum of its specimen was supposed to have led to his pursuit of the Clan Tulloch coronet out of sheer need of distraction. Now I knew that old Captain King of Clovelly owned the missing link, which he loved and kept dark. He was too much afraid of being bribed to part with it. His son was to be married as soon as he could get a ship. I posted to Clovelly, taking up at Bideford his intended daughter-in-law. We burst into his room. 'A bargain, Captain,' I said; 'the Painted Auk's egg for the barque *Nancinella*.' I produced the deed by which the *Nancinella* had been made over to me the morning before. At the same time I described poor Jervis's condition. King was compassionate and loved his son. He also felt the honour of a place in the Jervis cabinet for his Auk's egg. He unlocked his dresser drawer, and, with one long gaze, handed the egg to me.

"I was at Jervis's little house in Park Lane next day. He sat over the fire, heavy and dull. I clapped him on the shoulder. 'Let me see the eggs,' I said. With his usual courtesy, but

lethargically, he opened the cabinet. Drawer
after drawer he pulled out till he came to that
in which reposed the Auk eggs. Next to the
Little Auk was a vacant place. He turned for
some purpose to the table. I slipped the Painted
egg from its box in my side pocket, and set it in
the gap. Jervis was pushing back the drawer
half mechanically, when he started with a jubilant
exclamation. The whole man seemed to have
emerged from a chrysalis. He fluttered with no
less though a more radiant wonder than Leda's
lawful husband when he beheld Castor and Pollux
chipping their shell. I went out silently. The
next I heard of Jervis was the double news that
he had been reading a very learned paper at the
Linnean on the Painted Auk and its domestic
relations, and that he was gazetted to a brand-new
barony as Lord Oosis."

"Trivialities," he continued, "I dare say you
consider such incidents, my dear Partridge; and
no moral in them; but they divert me, and kill
time at once and money, both which commodities
are drugs in the market to us millionaires. However," he added, turning to me, "we must not
trouble this gentleman, who has the happiness not
to be one, with our shop." He held out his hand
to me as he spoke, obviously meaning that I was

leaving, as had not at all been my intention, and
not he.   But millionaires, even the meekest, have
a way with them which I for one find it not easy
to resist.   I took my dismissal as graciously as if
it had come from myself, and went away.   At the
same time I was very clear that it was not to be
the last I should see of a millionaire with Mr.
Stuckham's amiable dislike for the disappointment
of unfounded expectations.   That is the kind of
man with whom I always get on well.

CHAPTER X.

NIGHTMARE MASTERPIECES.

LIKE all busy men I have some spare time,
though my friends would never guess as much ;
and I spend it in auction rooms. I foresee a
criticism that it is an expensive fashion of ridding
oneself of leisure. Not for those who have as
little ready money as I, and as much resolution.
I bid for anything which catches my fancy. My
name is in the list of bidders for the Mandeville
Leonardo. I tried for all the best bits in the
Fountaine majolica. I was after the violin with
the three rows of black pearls in the Gillott sale.
If it had been knocked down to me, I meant to
have presented it to Joachim. I ran it up to three
guineas. That is my ordinary maximum. If I
can have a masterpiece in any branch of art for
three guineas, I take it ; if not, I wait. My gallery of masterpieces is not yet full. I am in no
hurry. There is as good fish in the sea as ever
came out of it.

Well, the last Saturday in May I occupied
my recognized corner in Christie's rooms at the

great Grubbins sale, when I noticed a sensation.
It was not produced by me.   Picture after picture, by Teniers, old and young, by Millais, by
Turner, by Landseer, by Rubens, by DeWint, by
Titian himself, was being put up, and was being
knocked down, one after another, to Mr. Alex-
ander Wix.   Everybody knows Wix the millionaire.   I know him — at a little distance.   There
he was, in his infamously old white hat, bidding
with cool decision.   Wix, it was plain, was collecting a gallery, and I was curious to trace the
direction his taste took.   I thought we might be
of mutual advantage, if I cared to part with a few
of my own treasures.   For, in truth and honour,
I could match at home the gems he was buying.

Such an assemblage of scarecrows has seldom
been seen.   They were authentic.   Scarecrows are
bound to be.   An ugly sham would have no
chance.   Wix is a shrewd man of business, who
has not scraped together a fortune out of tea-dust
in Mincing Lane to be put off with illegitimate
Correggios.   Every one of his new purchases had
an unimpeachable pedigree, and could vouch
Waagen, Smith, and Redford.   With that they
were as ragged a regiment as ever marched
through Coventry-street to Soho.   At the end
of the afternoon I lingered below till the happy

possessor was alone, but for the porter and me, with his stock of canvases. As he stood in the hall I ventured to approach and congratulate him. " Yes, a happy deliverance indeed," he answered, with a sigh. He had a slight difficulty in packing the mass in and upon a four-wheeler, and I offered my assistance. Somewhat to my surprise it was accepted. I seem to have a way with millionaires which they cannot resist any more than, as I have said, I can resist theirs. As the cab was endeavouring to start, I asked if I could be of service in hanging them. " Not exactly in hanging," was the reply, " though the operation is analogous. By all means come in if you be disengaged."

Mr. Wix's house is out of Wardour-street, a large and dismal tenement, which must have seen better days and worse. We unloaded the contents of the cab into the marble-paved hall, and the door was shut. " If you really care to help," said Mr. Wix, " I should be obliged if you would join me in carting these precious ruins into the back yard." I stared. " What!" said he, " you did not seriously suppose I bought them to keep?" I thought he had an American silver-mine man hidden up his sleeve, like a flea, and smiled a non-committal contortion of the lips and nose. Shouldering an enormous and gaunt Rembrandt, I walked him off into the hinder desolation. "Here, please, in the middle, on the tar-barrel," called my host. He was in his shirt-sleeves, and was armed with a long sharp carving-knife. With this he deftly sliced the painting out of its fittings, and arranged it, like a plaster, flat above the barrel. Another I hauled in, and another. All were huge gallery pictures, and all were shabby. Together they made, a round dozen of them, a thick slab of oil colors. By this time I had been reduced through surprise to a very feeble piece of docility, and simply stared. Finally, Mr. Wix recited, reverently enough, something which sounded like a verse from the funeral service, and, fetching a match-box, set the collection alight. In a quarter of an hour the product of a cheque for £1575 was a whiff of smoke with a very evil savour.

"You do not appear to understand, my dear Sir," said Mr. Wix, when the fumes were out of his nose and throat. "I believe I have remarked you in King-street, though you are not often a buyer. I fancied you were in the same line as myself. Perhaps you are not, and I may as well explain what mine is. When I had made my million I found as much trouble in knowing what to do with it as I have no doubt you find." I assured him I had found none as yet, for the sufficient reason that I had not the million. "Lucky man," said he; "you are spared an infinity of perplexity. 'How did I make mine?' you ask. I bought up an inventor's brains. Clever fellow; but improvident. Could not live upon £375 a year. I did; and had a bonus of a penny per cent, besides. Always behindhand he with butcher and baker. In County Asylum now, I am afraid. I got my million first. However, that is nothing to the purpose. Spending it, my friend; there's the rub.

"'Orchids,' you suggest. The ground is engaged. Besides, I have a conscience. Already the lesser mellisuga humming-bird has been starved out of existence. Every dasyphysis in Bahia, its sole food, has been grubbed away to supply the orchid houses at Hammersmith, Dorking, and Birmingham. I am not going to be an accessory to the extinction also of the phalangifer sub-species by collecting, as you seem inclined to advise, the pannimanoïds. I desire to be a benefactor, and not a destroyer.

"My first notion was that I would foster budding human genius. I very soon discovered that too many millionaire moles had been at the work. Every sucking genius who was not too deep in the earth, and plenty of counterfeits too, had been put carefully out to nurse. Search every garret, and all the benches in the Mall, summer night after summer night; I wager you will not discover a Chatterton, a Crabbe, or a Savage; not so much as a muse-struck Glasgow weaver on the tramp. No room that way for an out-of-work millionaire to find employment. But there is the dry-nurse, who, at any rate in Spain, tenderly nudges out of tedious existence decaying humanity, as well as the wet-nurse for infantile genius. I am that dry-nurse.

"In the course of my hunt after means for placing my million, I surveyed about all the contents of museums, libraries, and galleries, public or quasi-public, which are ticketed with famous names. I was introduced to the acquaintance of a vast body of their authors, painters, sculptors, writers, and men of science. Necessarily being all celebrated, they were most of them, the illustrious works and the illustrious workers, run to seed. The world, Sir, is cumbered with a prodigious and growing accumulation of intolerable and bewildering trash. Are not geniuses, you ask, rare? No, it is not that. The poor souls who never were geniuses are not to blame. The burnt-out geniuses are the nuisance. A genius is like an inverted pyramid. He starts with a work which is an inspiration. As soon as that has made its mark, his productions go on swelling till the minute supporting column groans under the overshadowing bulk above. Instead of a diminution of fertility the farther off he is from his source of inspiration, there is an inordinate exuberance. He inflicts the multiplied weight, not merely upon his generation, which could not complain of a burden emanating from itself, but upon innocent posterity.

" A work of art with a name attached to it is, alas, in ordinary circumstances, immortal. I now understand the kind purpose of Providence in having permitted the destruction of the Alexandrian Library; nay, of the Roman Empire. The object was in any manner to empty the unendurable charnel house of dead genius. A great poet's fancy may be in a state of petrifaction. Do merciful publishers purge their editions of his excruciating lumps of rhyme? A painting may be mildewed, moth-eaten, faded in all its tints. Did you ever hear of its quiet extinction? It may have been still-born; it must not be buried, because it has been signed by a Landseer, a Wilkie, or a Rubens. Without a spark of light from its birth, it is embalmed, and claims to perpetuate its mummy's grin at a down-trodden public.

" During my searches for subjects of patronage in galleries and at auctions I had suffered tortures from impaled carcasses of genius. As at length my vocation dawned upon me, I had something of the feeling of a hangman of domestic proclivities, when he recognizes, as he fastens the noose for the homicidal burglar, the wretch whom he saw by moonlight shooting, for mere revolver practice, his favourite tom-cat on the garden wall. I was only afraid that my philanthropy might be a veil for personal vindictiveness. If it be, may I be pardoned for the sake of the certain deliverance I have accomplished for my kind from many and many an incubus! Do you remember the big Michael Angelo I tore from the covetous grasp of the Director of the National Gallery? Think of the effect of the installation of that dreadful object in the heart of the collection! If only I had lived in Sir Charles Eastlake's time! I dare say you have sometimes wondered, like the rest, where the Reynolds, the Mrs. Gwynne, which I was rumoured to have purchased for £2000 to present to Trafalgar Square, really went. Would you care to see a sample? Here is a genuine relic — a bit of the poor dear skeleton's fingers. Connoisseurs may thank my backyard for a release from a perilous trap for fictitious or factitious enthusiasm.

"But pray do not imagine that I deal only in pictures. All is fish that comes to my net, so that I rescue the guileless public from the shame of spurious raptures. For example, I learnt the other day that our poet, Troubutt, was on the point of issuing a new volume. I am an old friend of Troubutt's. Down I hurried to his country house. He was gone to bed. On the hall table I saw a bulbous parcel addressed to an eminent firm. It was to be registered the first thing in the morning. Not a moment was to be lost. I sent up to say I must see him that night. He dressed, and came down into his study. 'Troubutt,' I said, 'you must show me the new poems. I cannot sleep till I have seen them.' He was flattered and agitated, at one and the same time. 'Would you not prefer to read them in print?' he asked. 'Goodness gracious, no!' I cried; 'I hope things have not come to that pass yet. You must read them to me yourself.' Poets love to read their own verses aloud, and always read atrociously. But I had an object, and it was worth a sacrifice.

"Troubutt undid the bundle, and began. I had guessed what it would be, and yawned a deep sigh of relief at our escape. The whole was nothing but a brassy echo of the man as he was before the vein of poetry had been worked out. The public, however, would have taken it all upon trust, and have diluted the strong liquor of the past with these watery dregs. 'A thousand pounds, Troubutt,' I said, 'for the lot. Rigsdon would give no more, and you keep your reputation unimpaired.' Troubutt is at bottom a sensible fellow. While his poetry has gone off into prose, his critical acumen has improved. He understands very well that his verses are now nothing but verses. Readily enough he accepted my terms, on condition that I said guineas. Shaking hands, I assured him that he would slumber sounder for the arrangement; and I caught the last train up.

"Next morning I spoilt my coffee, and finally set the chimney on fire, with smouldering fozy ballads. If Wordsworth had possessed in his last thirty years a friend like me! Still, though it was simply Troubutt, it was a good stroke of business; and I wish I could have bought up the man for once and all. Unfortunately, a popular poet's estimate of himself is high, and I have so much to do with my money.

"Preachers and politicians are cheaper. I have put a golden muzzle with little difficulty on several superannuated members of both classes. People have disputed why the senior member for the Pumpkin Boroughs never speaks in the House now. I know, and my bankers too. His fame is dear to his countrymen and to his wife. I have arranged with him, whose income is not what it ought to be, that he shall keep that fame unspoilt.

"I wonder, by the by, if you ever heard how I purchased in one lot a whole committee of the Royal Inductive Society. One afternoon I happened to hear that a committee was sitting to report upon an alleged discovery of the convertibility of the laws of organic and inorganic existence. The result had been reached after five years of patient inquiry by that shy but brilliant student, Robert Georges. The Inductive Society had nominated a selection of its senior leading members — all authors of Ellesmere Prize treatises — to sit upon the discovery. There was no danger that they would be without interest in the question, it being notorious that the new conclusions contradicted all on which the renown acquired by the committee-men half a century before mainly rested. For Georges much depended on the form of the report. He had a young family, to which he was, out of his laboratory, intensely devoted. If the report, which he saturninely took for granted would be adverse, should be truculent, I had reason to believe he had resolved to renounce this most promising branch of investigation. He had been offered the very lucrative post of hop auscultator at Grain's Brewery, Limited, and had provisionally accepted.

"I was intimately acquainted with the seniors of the Inductive Society, and could have written out their report in advance. On the decisive afternoon I went to the rooms, sent in an octogenarian French savant's name, and was admitted. My unexpected appearance disturbed the members present, I could perceive, though they were civil enough. 'Gentlemen,' I said, 'you are preparing to sum up against the convertibility theory.' They could not deny their intention, which the boldest of them endeavoured apologetically to justify. I cut him short, and continued: 'You must feel that you are not competent to consider the question independently. You were excellent in your generation, to which you properly belonged, and belong still. At the same time you ought to be sensible that you have lost all faith in the infinite progressiveness of science, and that you think its mobility a nuisance.' They assented sorrowfully, and with dumb signs. 'Now,' I went on, 'I propose that you retire. Here is a deed formally drawn up, by which you engage all of you to do nothing in science, orally or in writing, but comment on and re-edit your own invaluable volumes in the Ellesmere Series. On my part,

I engage to purchase from each an annual edition of one thousand copies of his particular treatise; the entire issue to be at my sole disposition. This secures to every one a comfortable income, and innocent occupation on his own venerable hypotheses. Will you accept? Inclusive terms — the committee at a lump sum?'

"One elderly philosopher stood out for a while, for the sake, he alleged, of the eternal verities. He wanted to know what I meant to do with the Ellesmere impressions; but I refused to disclose the name of the butterman. He haggled for leave to cut up in the Transactions the revised edition of Cocker. I was firm, not that anybody probably would have been the wiser for his printed lucubrations. His brethren conjured him to assent, and I soothed his conscience by letting him loose against the Commons Preservation Society. In general, they were not only willing, but thankful. They knew they could not trust themselves, and their antiquated prejudices. It was not a cheap affair; but I have never repented of the expense of muzzling a knot of respectable bygone celebrities, who had long squatted down upon science, and blocked up its thoroughfares. I wish I could as easily stop the mouths of divers Judges, naval and military theorists, journalists, novelists, and

political economists. So far as I have gone, I
should like to know where you would find a
more truly and profitably benevolent an employment for a million than mine."

I acknowledged it would be hard, if not impossible. As, on my walk home, I passed Burlington
House and the National Gallery — from which re-
spectively the eloquent President and the reticent
Director happened to be issuing — and the Houses
of Parliament, and Westminster Abbey, in the pre-
cincts of which Convocation was at the time sitting, I regretted cordially that there had been no
series of Wixes for several centuries past to weed
Church, and State, and Art, of the works of geniuses whose genius has unfortunately got addled
or pumped out. An occasional glance at my own
little collection of Dutch masterpieces strengthens
rather than weakens the impression. I sometimes
speculate on the possible effect of an inspection of
them upon Mr. Wix. He certainly has burnt better or worse.

CHAPTER XI.

THE possibility thus suggested had the curious result of inflaming my taste for paying attention to merit out at elbows. It was happy for me. I made a valuable and remunerative acquaintance. One morning I was at some well-known auction rooms, to which I should be sorry to attract excessive and disturbing notice. I will therefore simply describe them as somewhere within a parallelogram inclosed by Bond-street, Tottenham Court Road, Fetter Lane, and the Victoria Embankment. I was bidding up to my habitual figure for a Sheraton commode, and, as is not unusual with me, losing it. At the close of the sale an old gentleman in new clothes, which manifestly were all of them misfits, came up to me. He introduced himself as the successful purchaser. " Sorry to interfere with you, Sir," he said ; " but I see we are in the same public line, and, you or I, it cannot matter. The thing is safe, at all events, at my little place."

I responded civilly that it was the fortune of war, and I wished him joy. The particular specimen was, I admitted, interesting, though, I feared, not without defects. He appeared then to apprehend that he had mistaken my vocation, as he had. Having noticed me bidding on many previous occasions, he had jumped to the conclusion that we were on the same mission. "But possibly," he said, "you are of my friend Wix's opinion — a fine courage has Wix — that dead curios tell no tales. I am not quite equal to that." I saw that I had tapped a fresh millionaire spring. So, though I did not in the least understand the character of his vocation, I spoke so enthusiastically round and about it as to arouse his kindness. "Would you care," he asked, "to visit my collection?" I responded ecstatically, and no time, he remarked, being so good as the present, he arranged to meet me at Liverpool-street that afternoon at three. On a card he gave me I read that his name was Alfred Splotch. I was to take a return ticket, second class, to Burial Farm Station, and to look out for him near the luggage truck.

Following his directions, I encountered him in the midst of a pile of heavy packages, which were being tumbled very disrespectfully into the train. We were soon at our destination, where, beside a cavalcade of hearses, a black trap was awaiting Mr. Splotch, with a waggon and carter. Mr.

Splotch ordered the man to bring the things on, and, putting me into the dog-cart, drove off. About a couple of miles away, a little beyond the end of the Necropolis wall, we came to a rather large, dead-flat inclosure, which I suppose would have to be called a park. It was surrounded by a carefully stuccoed wall, so smooth as to be incapable of supporting a single tuft of moss. At the entrance was an architectural lodge, St. Pancras Church in miniature.

The gate was flung open solemnly by a man in character, the fac-simile of a parish beadle. We drove along a straight gravel road, terminated by the ugliest mock Palladian Portland-cement mansion I have ever had the unhappiness to see. A butler in black, like a mute, stood on the steps, at once sly and pompous, cringing and despotic. My host was a mild little man, and his servants treated him accordingly. He informed me that dinner would be ready in half an hour, and he met me to the minute at the drawing-room door. He did not, he explained, sit much in that apartment, preferring the staircase. The dining-room was like the rest of the house. The dinner-table was furnished with a costly service, — epergnes with the camels, silver camels, for flowers, and all the excruciating splendours of fifty years ago, against which the Church Catechism superfluously warns us.

Very soon after dinner, Mr. Splotch, when I declined the decanters, rose and said : " But we have to see the collection while the light serves." The house was wide and spreading, and the top floor had been converted into one immense lumber depository. My nerves, disciplined as they have been, never experienced a stranger effect. I have been a looker into shop windows all my life ; and here were all their horrors come back upon me.

It was a huge gathering of upholstery monstrosities, and every one I seemed to know. The hideous carved oak cabinet which had offended me for years in Regent-street stood there. Here was the big glass chandelier, which for a century nobody would buy in Oxford-street. Here again was the carpet which looked like a noisy trouser pattern in the windows of the Oriental depot. There were wardrobes, wardrobes, wardrobes, and still wardrobes. There were the odious Anglo-Japanese teacups, with the grinning nightmares depicted upon them, which had been trundled round the last dozen international exhibitions. There were the Empire clocks, which the first Napoleon used to say half reconciled him to St. Helena, where there were none. There was everything which had never been beautiful, and had once been expensive.

I turned to Mr. Splotch in wonder and pity. He understood my mute sympathy. "Yes," he said, "I flatter myself I have succeeded to a certain point. I do what I can. Wix is luckier. He buys carcasses, and has not the trouble of reminding them that they are dead. A Giorgione with nine-tenths of the paint rubbed off has earned the repose of the grave, and he gives it its due. He saves what has been beautiful from the cruel irony of admiration for qualities it no longer has.

"My lot is humbler, though, I hope, not without its use. You see, when I made my million, all the philanthropists were down upon me. They forced me to admit that I owed something to humanity, if not to sweetness and light. For father and brothers and self to have saved a million or two out of oleomargarine does rather stink in the nostrils later on, as one sits in the family pew over the family vault. But I said to myself that there are worse impostures than butterine, and better objects than the maintenance of the staff of the Cosmopolitan Refuge for Nasal Pimples. Though it took me long to discover an alternative, it revealed itself at last.

"Everybody must have observed a fatal law of industrial economy. When a thing has been made, it is bound to live and to sell. Look at

this house. Can you match it for effrontery of
ugliness? It is as bombastic as a cochin china
cock, as inconvenient as the Law Courts, and as
smelly and insanitary as a Pall Mall Club. All
the world knows that it is Sir Turveydrop Jones's
ne plus extra, and it looks like it, and smells like
it. Well, here it is, and somebody has to live in
it. You cannot pull down a mansion twenty years
old, which contains half a square mile of best
cement, and fifty perches of timber, warranted
useless for any other purpose. Already in its
short career it has sent two builders into the
Bankruptcy Court, one father of a family into
the County Lunatic Asylum, and three sets of
innocent children — an only son, twin girls, and a
paralytic baby — into handsome brick vaults in
the neighbouring cemetery.

"For the eighth time it was standing empty,
and a bargain. Happening to be driving past, in
the cemetery omnibus, I saw a respectable family
man gazing at the funereal board. I saw that he
saw somebody had to take it, and that he was
meditating reluctantly whether it were not he.
I am without wife, child, or maiden aunt, and,
after a hurried calculation, perceived that I could
abide the ordeal with less damage. Moreover,
there might even be a certain harmony between

the place and some sticks and things I had begun
to gather about me. The other candidate, who
had just made up his mind in the affirmative, set,
I remarked, his face towards the agent's office
while I was reflecting. He walked about as nim-
bly as if he were on his way to see himself tied
up at Tyburn, and I speedily overtook him. By
the time he arrived I had signed an agreement
to purchase. Never did I behold an air of more
relief in a man's face than when he heard his self-
sacrifice was not required. Then he gazed at me
with admiration. 'Better I than you,' I smiled
back. I entered at once, only stopping to pick
up a workhouse beadle, the tyrant of St. Mary,
Triplethwaite, and a family butler, with a character manifestly forged, who had marred the domestic tranquillity of six servants' halls, and bullied
an earl and three baronets into a state of scared
imbecility.

" Ever since I have been furnishing, and am
not dissatisfied, on the whole, with the result.
Those epergnes, for instance, at dinner; did you
ever come across any more afflicting specimens of
the silversmith's art? Here, where it cannot be
denied that they are perfectly in keeping, they
work little mischief. Examine this cupboard,
with the Japanese lacquer. It is true Japanese

work, in a sense.   It was actually constructed in
the vicinity of Nangasaki, from a pattern of the
South Kensington School of Design despatched to
Japan.   A tradition is current that the Japanese
artist first employed committed the happy despatch.   He needed Nirvana, he said, after a
twelvemonth of British fancies.   It had to be
completed by a second, with amaurosis in the left
eye.   The right he kept bandaged.

"When it arrived in Bond-street somebody had
to buy it.   A syndicate was being got up to ac-
quire it for Bethnal Green, when I leaped into the
chasm.   Locked up here, even such a thing is comparatively harmless.   I have heard it said that it
would be kinder to chop such things into firewood,
or put them into Mr. Eassie's patent crematorium,
after Wix's method.   You cannot.   One has no
more power to burn a cabinet, with all its timber,
carving, veneer, ivory, and buhl, sound as a bell,
than one has the power to burn my butler, much
as one might like to do both.   They insist on
living out their lawful span, which is by no means
short.   The most I can do is to keep them close
in Graveyard Hall.   The same with the house.
Once there was a hope that damp was in the
walls.   A mere delusion!   Nothing better, alas,
than a choked-up waste-pipe against the house."

By this the light had faded, and I did not choose to be longer in such gruesome company. We went downstairs, and I bid good-night to my host, who would gladly have detained me for the sake of society. Refusing his offer of the trap, I walked to the station. The entire length of the cemetery wall I shivered at the recollection of the spectacle at which I had assisted. Still, I wished the space in the establishment had been ampler for some distinctive varieties of human, as well as artistic, life. Within my own circle many persons are numbered, vigorous, sturdy, and likely to live as long as myself, whom — or at any rate their neighbours — a permanent enjoyment of Mr. Splotch's hospitality would precisely suit. No statutory authority, however, I believe, at present can be specified, under which people may be shut up for being clumsy, awkward, and in bad taste. I am not even sure that Parliament would consent to the necessary legislation, though Splotch should undertake to supply additional accommodation for the business.

In any case he has done a good turn to somebody. I had grown, as I lately hinted, rather tired of my own collection of carved and pictorial curiosities. As no fine-art auctioneer — wheels within wheels — they are all jealous — would accept a reasonable commission for its dispersion, I hired a West End corner shop for a month. There I displayed all my able-bodied gems. — My Old Masters I knew would not suit Splotch. — I spied him from the back parlour, staring in at the door with the look upon his mild face of having come upon a good thing. A friend of mine, of jovial family aspect, meanwhile was, by arrangement, examining articles as minutely as if he were on the point of buying wholesale for a boudoir and schoolroom. Two days later I received a note from my shopman. The stock had been taken en bloc, on most favourable terms for the vendor. Inclosed was a handsome cheque signed " Alfred Splotch."

CHAPTER XII.

THE SELF-INDULGENT MILLIONAIRE.

I DO not quite know how it is, but I have lately found the supply of millionaires who spend on the public growing scanty. Though millionaires in general are as plentiful as blackberries, my experience for some time past has lain chiefly among those who spend upon themselves. Probably it is mere accident. Millionaires hunt in packs. If you fall in with one, the chances are that you will come across a score of others of the same class. At present I am on the selfish line.

I am simply stating a fact. Far be it from me to insinuate that a millionaire may not be thoroughly good and conscientious, though he spend according to his own individual pleasure. A few days ago I actually heard a millionaire, James Heskethson, contending that such a principle of expenditure is absolutely more virtuous. We had been dining at Greenwich, and he was to pay. I took the opportunity of a break after the coffee was brought, to inquire what he was doing with his million. He had told me how his uncle,

Daniel Barker, had made it, by extracting the oil, through hydraulic pressure, from empty sardine-tins. Naturally, I commenced by assuming that, as Barker's heir, he had taken, or would take, to philanthropy. "No," he said; "I do not hold with philanthropy in any shape. My fixed belief is that the reason of half the millionaire charity-mongering is the desire of men to disguise from themselves that they are failures. Our fellows do no good by running Board schools against one another for Senior Wranglers, by their Sunday buttonholes for Shoreditch costermongers, their turtle-soup kitchens, and their Caxton, Elzevir, and Aldine reading-rooms. On the contrary, they eat the heart out of the community's independence. Only, it cannot be proved. The secretaries and managers declare it is all a magnificent success, and the millionaire benefactor is able to swallow the flattery down. He has an illuminated parchment with votes of thanks inscribed upon it, to demonstrate how profitably he has invested his money. When he spends on himself, he cannot help finding out what an ass he is. If we knew how to get rid of our income on ourselves, without too ridiculous a fiasco, do you imagine we should go outside?

"I fancy I have learnt, and I do not mind telling

you my plan.   As you are aware, I am hardly a downright, proper millionaire.   Perhaps that is how I succeed better in living up to my income than most of us.   A truly authentic millionaire must be the work of his own hands.   Nobody ever calls a duke a millionaire, though he have £300,000 a year, and lazily let it pile itself up. A veritable millionaire has a million to spend because he has made it, and he can do what he likes with his own.   But because he has made it, and it is his, he is just the man not to spend it on himself.   He made it by not spending on himself, and he is unable to unmake it in that way.   I am under no such disqualification.   My million came to me, as I have intimated, from my good old uncle Barker, Barker the philanthropist. He left it me.

"That is, he did not, technically, leave it me. Indeed, he had vowed that a scapegrace like me should not have a penny, and he had a will drawn, by which all was to go to the foundation of a hospital for religious monomaniacs.   His fortune had been in railway stocks; but a month after he had executed the will, he bought a job lot of ten King's New River shares at an auction.   Then he died.   He had forgotten that New River shares are realty, and that the Mortmain

Acts forbid the endowment of religious mono-
mania. Consequently the hospital took nothing,
and I inherited.

"I knew how wrong my uncle had gone with
his charitable fads. I determined to go quite the
other way. My maxim always has been that
charity begins at home; and I am home. If a
man is incompetent to buy happiness and comfort
for himself, he is not likely to bring happiness and
comfort through his money to others. My principles in this respect are indisputably correct. The
difficulty was to apply them in practice. In the
first place I was fettered by my descent. Though
my paternal ancestry, of the sporting squire sort,
was all right, there was on the maternal side, the
great scrivener side, saving blood in me. The
money itself did not help me. It had never been
taught, like an old family property, to run itself
out.

"Thus, I had at first several very bad quarters
of an hour before I hit upon the correct course.
I permitted myself to be elected President of the
Home for Erastian Inebriates, and Vice-President
of the Institute of Aural Gnostics and Neo-Ther-
mal Hypochondriacs. The one thing to be pleaded
in extenuation of the folly is that I held back
my Presidential and Vice-Presidential donations

till I should be able to comprehend the benefit I, who am neither an afflicted Gnostic nor a heated Hypochondriac, was to derive. As I have never yet comprehended it, the cheques have not been despatched. The experience of other charities which have pressed dignities upon me has been similar. They now leave me alone. In the Charity Directory I am marked, ' No effects.'

" But my adherence to principle added to my perplexities in the employment of my dividends. I had cut off some of the most easily available conduit-pipes. Anybody can say he means to spend his income on himself. It is more readily said than done. It is not generally understood how strictly moderate is the sum which, in ordinary circumstances, a man lays out on himself. Examine your accounts minutely; reckon up all you spend on your personal self, and you will perceive that it amounts to a small proportion alone of your total disbursements.

" The other day I was inspecting the accounts of the young Duke of Eastham. There has not been a more racketty lad. Yet, out of the £80,000 he has been annually spending from an income of £50,000, his own expenditure does not exceed a bare £7000. I have a trifle more than was his Grace's rental before the agricultural depression.

My figure may be £60,000, or, in bonus years, perhaps £80,000. But of this I ascertained that I had been in the habit of spending on myself some £2000. I felt this could not but be preposterously wrong, and that it was in truth the effect of a fraud upon oneself. A rich man finds it extremely hard to divest himself of the notion that things he wants have a sort of fixed price. He will not pay for them more than persons with a fiftieth part of his money pay. I broke through that superstition, and immediately the course was clear. As soon as I had arrived at the conclusion that my duty to myself is to pay exactly as much as is necessary to satisfy my wants, I ceased to have the least trouble with plethoric bank balances.

"Shortly after my development of the practical millionaire's art of spending, I turned into Christie's, which was in a state of suppressed emotion. A picture, a little bit of a thing, was being held up above the table prior to the opening of biddings. I had never bought a painting except "Cherry Ripe" in a Christmas Number. Now, I fell in love with one. I meant to have it. Several dealers in the room were resolved too, especially Thibagg. The biddings opened, after a humourous offer of £3 by somebody unknown, with one of £1000 by McTavish. I let him and Thibagg spar at one another to £5000, and then I took them up. On went Thibagg, with his false front teeth so hard clenched that he could not speak out his biddings, and had to nod them. He knew that I was engaged to luncheon at 1.30, and must go, leaving him, as he hoped, a fair field. I went, though not before I had slipped a blank cheque into the clerk's hand, and whispered to him, 'Buy.'

"At two I received at my friend's chambers a pencilled message from King-street, 'Yours at twenty thousand.' In the course of the afternoon I was at the rooms. My principal antagonist was there also, and congratulated me heartily. I was, he thought, a valuable new recruit of the lucrative flock of connoisseur sheep. I have never repented of my purchase, but, in fact, since that day I have bought nothing. It has not happened to me to fall in love with another canvas. 'What was the name of the painter?' you ask. Well, the odd thing was that I did not know when I bid. I was told afterwards that it is by Raffaelle, the Fitz-Stephen Madonna, *alias* the Madonna della Bacciola.

"I have been told that I paid extravagantly for the meadow in front of my cottage at Chiswick.

The cottage suits me. No, it is not freehold; a tenancy at will, from year to year. The landlord will not turn out so improving an occupant, and Topsey Hall sickened me of permanent ties. In front was a vacant plot, in different ownership, half an acre or so. I did not want the ground. My garden is big enough for me. If it were not, I hate crossing a road. But it overlooks, not my house, but my bowling green at the corner. One morning I saw a board with a notice that this eligible ripe frontage, eighty rods, two yards, one foot and a half, more or less, was to be sold at the Auction Mart on May 6. I glanced at the calendar. I had been from home, and came back very late the night before. This was May 6, and it was twelve o'clock, an hour before the sale. Fortunately I was dressed. I jumped into a Hansom, which, by a happy accident, had just landed a fare opposite. I promised the man a guinea if he got me to Tokenhouse Yard by one. He earnt his money.

"The conditions were being read over. The first bid was £75. I called out £300. The auctioneer stared, and a clerk came during the pause and civilly inquired my name. I gave him my card, which he carried to the rostrum. The auctioneer knew his trade, and in an absent way

read it out.   Forthwith the whole roomful of
land agents woke up.   The biddings rose by leaps
and bounds, till I was pronounced the purchaser
for £6500.   A friendly stranger remonstrated with
me on the idiotic freak of giving sixty times the
value of the field.   But I wanted it, I told him,
and what more reason could be offered?   What
could it matter whether the sum were £70 or
£7000, if I wanted the eighty perches and did not
want the money?   Probably it would have been
£10,000, if a particle of city dust had not irritated
my throat, and produced a hesitating little cough
at the £6500.   My opponents were startled.
They were afraid I might stop if they capped me,
and, for a joke, plant them with the half-acre at
their disposal.   To me it made little difference,
provided I kept bricks and mortar off.   It is horrid to be overlooked when you are preparing for
a scattering dash at the jack.

"It is possible," proceeded Mr. Heskethson,
"that you may not understand so easily why I
spent £5000 in fetching Ivan Zlavoski out of
Eastern Siberia.   A drunken old rascal is Zlavoski,
and costs me an income in brandy.   You presume
it was humanity.   No, it was not humanity.   The
fact is, I admire Turgeneff; and Zlavoski, in the
novelist's best period, was his amanuensis.   Turge-

neff, I discovered, never really wrote in Russian. He dictated his stories in French, leaving Zlavoski to translate them into the vernacular. From that Parisian booksellers' hacks have retranslated them into French. I wished to have them read back to me into the first-hand French. For the purpose I stole my Pole out of his Asiatic exile. You think the outlay extravagant; but you must pardon me for saying that, as you are acquainted with '*les Cossaques*' only in third-hand French, you are scarcely a judge.

"I am prepared to find that you set down as equally extravagant my payment the other day of Denning's Stock Exchange differences. True, it was £15,000, and Denning, as you say, is no relation. But for the last dozen years, ever since he married, he has gone to his and my club at half-past four, and played a rubber or two rubbers, shilling points, before walking home with me. He lives a stone's throw off my London house. If I had not paid for him, he must have ceased to be a member of the Stock Exchange. His other creditors would have gazetted him a bankrupt. He might have gone to join his brother's firm at Rangoon. At all events, his insolvency would have vacated his membership of the Areopagus. Where should I have been? What should

I have done for a partner? Who would have walked across the Park after dark with me? I call the arrangement cheap at £15,000, particularly when one does not know what to do with the money.

"I have been laughed at, I am aware, for giving £10 to the skipper of the fishing-smack *Lucy* for a patent bootjack, when I was on my way in my steam-yacht *Elba* to Iceland. Five shillings, I know as well as you, is the price. But patent bootjacks are not to be dredged up in the German Ocean, and it is miserable to me to be without one. The skipper of the *Lucy* had taken one to sea for luck, and he appraised his luck at £10. I have never felt the money loss. My maxim is, make sure what you want, and don't lose it for a few pounds one side or the other. You will economize the whole and more, if money be an object, by being careful not to spend on things you don't want.

"I am not a man to require much. Only, what I like I like seriously. Last Friday I had an engagement in the neighbourhood of York. When I reached Euston the train was moving from the platform. No, I had not lost it; I never lose trains; I can't, for I never look at Bradshaw to see when there will be one; I just go to the

station whenever it is convenient. On this occasion I should have had to wait two hours. Two
hours in and about Euston Square! Not possible.
I ordered a train. At what cost? you ask. I do
not know. It was entered, I suppose, in my bill
for specials at the Universal Railway Booking
Office.

"My one principle is to spend my income —
and I nearly manage that, not . quite — so as
to procure as much as possible from it, for myself. I cannot help being misconstrued sometimes.
For instance, one of you writing fellows made a
wonderful mess in trying to explain my part in
the revival of the Durston Sugar Refinery. You
recollect the failure of the refinery two years ago,
and its as sudden resurrection under the same
management. John Durston, a first-rate chemist,
has, you know, patented a process of aërating
sugar. He has built for his workmen a model
village half a mile from a crazy old manor house
of mine, where I stay two or three months at odd
times in a year. I like it, I verily believe, mainly
on account of Durstonville. Such merry children
— polite too; such tidy housewives; such cabbages
and cabbage roses.

"I was at the Manor in June, 1888, and took
my evening stroll to Durstonville. I never saw

anything so gloomy. Groups of workmen standing stupidly about. No cricket on the green.
Children and mothers crying and nagging. No
silken threads of smoke from the kitchen chimneys. Newspaper reading is not one of my pleasures, though I sometimes buy an outer sheet of
the *Times* in the Parliamentary vacations. So I
had heard nothing of John Durston's boom in
petroleum, or of its collapse. Foolish fellow! not
content with sugar, he had gone into the application of petroleum as nap for hats in place of
silk. Texture, look, everything much better.
Would at once have superseded silk hats. But
the Prince's sudden resolution, after the fate
of his new silk at the Botanical Gardens Rose
Parade, never more to wear anything but felt left
nothing to supersede. Silk hats and petroleum
hats became equally a drug. Though aërated
sugar remained as profitable as ever, Durstonville
could not carry Napville as well as itself. Durston had been compelled, I was told, to go into
liquidation. The receiver had closed the Durstonville mills from lack of capital to work them.

"Day after day there was the same sad scene,
and worse on Sunday, when the vicar preached
on Rizpah, and the sores of Job, and the beauty
of chastisement. I could stand it no longer. As

it would have been most annoying for me to abridge my stay at the Manor, I called upon Durston on the Monday morning, and took him and the receiver into Richston, to the bank. With the aid of my solicitor I made it clear that I was to be answerable for Durston's eventual solvency. If there should be a deficit on the two businesses, when the creditors met, it was to be my affair. The bank gladly supplied cash to set the works going again, and by Tuesday Durstonville was as bright and cheerful as ever. That was what I wanted. It is not worth my while to have a slatternly, famished, discontented village within hearing of my dinner-gong.

" The nuisance was that the Richston poet put me into a sonnet as a philanthropist. A London journalist too, on the hunt for a theme, wrote a dithyrambic leader on millionaires as they might be, with me cast for the hero. Fancy, the stuff, and about me! As if to turn me into greater ridicule, I had, I am almost ashamed to mention, my pleasant Arcadia restored to me for nothing. The Prince, you remember, perjured himself when an admirer of Durston's showed him a Napville petrolard. He resumed chimney tops wildly. They could not be too glossy for him, and the fashionable world instantly flooded Napville with orders.

In three months from my Monday visit to Richston bank the receiver was removed both from
Napville and Durstonville.   All my advances,
though I had not minded whether they were
unpaid or not, were returned to me to the last
farthing, with the ugliest service of silver plate
that human eye ever contemplated, by way of
interest."

I had never, I told Mr. Heskethson, met a millionaire of more common sense.   Though he heard
me without immoderate elation, he let me understand that this was his own experience and feeling.   But I mentioned that one thing surprised
me.   A million, I know, is a good round sum,
and is of the cut-and-come-again order.   If it be
given time it is able and willing to satisfy all
reasonable, and some unreasonable, demands.   In
ordinary circumstances there is no difficulty in
complying with the condition I have specified.
Thus, a million, when it is directed by its owner
to minister to the public, lets its objects understand that they have to abide its convenience.
They cannot help themselves, and he does not
mind.   It is different when a millionaire requires
his million to serve himself.   Obviously he is not
inclined to wait; and I clearly perceived from the
account Mr. Heskethson had given me that he,

for example, was not in the habit of waiting. I was curious to learn whether, in fact, he had to give due notice, or his million dispensed with it.

He saw my difficulty, but assured me it was imaginary. "Money," he said, "is like a horse, or a wife"—he is a bachelor—"and is very much what its proprietor expects it to be. If he treat it as if it had a right to long and ceremonious notice before it is put in harness, it will very soon grow sluggish and sulky. I have always been fond of trying its paces. I was born to prevent it from ossifying. With me it understands that it has to be very much on the alert. I believe in ready money; and it is as ready when it is in my cheque book as when it is in my purse.

"You look at me as if you pitied my million for having so capricious and hard a taskmaster. I am entirely the reverse. I am not one of the millionaires whose cash is like a servant hired to wait on a single gentleman, with no warning that the amiable bachelor is sole uncle to six large families of nephews and nieces. I do not order my banknotes in a hundred diverse directions, to draw teeth at a Dental Hospital, to make beef soup, to be a truss, or a cripple's crutch, to panel a national art gallery with simpering antique saints, at which nobody looks. It has solely to satisfy me ; and satisfy me it shall and must, without wool-gathering. In my honest judgment there is no cause to condole with it for having to gratify my few and simple wants, instead of being hustled about Retreats for Widowed Dogs and Refuges for Cats with Tails out of Curl."

CHAPTER XIII.

THE RESPECTABLE MILLIONAIRE.

I belong to the Periander Club. In handbooks to London it is described as a Constitutional Club. The reason is not so much that its members have a particular political bias as that they are all respectable gentlemen. That is why I belong to it, though I, or my banker, who has kindly accepted an order to pay the amount annually, finds the subscription heavy. Generally its members, I should say, are well off, but not too well off. They have nothing about them offensively rich. It is not a club where it is easy to know people familiarly. It is too respectable for that. One may see them every day for thirty years, smoke with them, play whist with them, dine with them — in the coffee-room — repeat the evening paper to them — and never know where they live, if anywhere. I have a large acquaintance among them of this sort. But I have come most in contact with Bugbrooke. That is, I have seen more, and known, till the other evening, less of him, than of any of the rest.

One night, at the end of November, a Sunday night, I turned into the smoking-room. No Periander men, as a rule, go into the smoking-room on a Sunday. They are, by courtesy, supposed to have family bosoms to retire into on that, if no other day. Still, the room happened to have an inmate. It was Bugbrooke. The night was dark and foggy, with snow in the air. For a time we solemnly smoked opposite one another, and alternately remarked on the superiority of the Continental methods of dealing with a snowfall. At last, feeling such society, taken dry, somewhat oppressive, I rang for a glass of whiskey and water. Bugbrooke copied me. Then suddenly a veil seemed to be lifted, and he grew confidential. Perhaps it appeared to him futile to wrap himself in the morgue of a respectable reserve, when every waiter in the Club knew he was smoking and drinking toddy on a Sunday night in Piccadilly. He began to talk of private and personal affairs; and from a casual remark he let drop, I discovered that he was a millionaire.

One does not expect somehow to find millionaires at the Periander, respectable as we are. I expressed my gratification at his presence among us, giving by the way a little dissertation on the utility of millionairing and its pleasures. I do not pretend

that I said anything very new, but I hope I said it
neatly and in good taste. Bugbrooke received my
remarks with a deprecatory shake of the head.
"No," he said, after a pause; "I am not conscious
that I made my million for the reasons you state;
nor do I spend it as you inform me your other
millionaire friends are accustomed to spend theirs.
I am only a commonplace men's millionaire;
though possibly, as, to judge by your observations,
that is not the ordinary kind, you may care to
hear something concerning it.

"To begin, I was not always well off, as probably you have been." That, by the way, is so like
millionaires. They know I am not one of them.
Consequently, they infer I must have been born in
the purple, and never had occasion, as they, to toil
and spin. However, he went on: "I had my own
way to make, and very hard I found the pavement, both to lay and to run on, when it was laid.
Not wood, or even decent macadam by any means.
I bought up a row of little houses, resting on solid
foundations of dry sewage, with the few hundreds
my wife, a cheap tailor's daughter, brought me,
not to speak of a temper. I set up bakers' shops,
and perfumed the neighbourhood with alum. I
lent money, and was not wickedly cheated of my
pound of flesh. I pinched and screwed all round.

"For forty years I did not know what it was to eat a slice from a prime joint. I was always on the search for cheap pennyworths. I did not remind a customer that he had reckoned a half-crown as a florin when he was handing in silver for a bill. I slipped a threepenny-piece into the plate at church — or chapel, as it was for me then — so artfully that it was covered by my neighbour's self-glorious shilling. I walked three yards within a two-mile radius that a cabman should spend on me the fullest amount of horseflesh. I sold the bed from under a widow and orphans in right of the dead insolvent husband's bill of sale. When I was honest I went near enough to dishonesty to look it in the face across the party-wall. I should have liked to be fraudulent, if there had been no danger of the Old Bailey. I was shabby to my neighbours, to all who dealt with me, to my wife, to myself — to myself shabbiest of all, cruelly, barbarously shabby. I swear, when I think of all the meannesses I committed against myself, I shed tears of shame, pity, and wrath. I could beat, maul, scratch, and worry the man I was to poor me, whenever there was the faintest hope of stealing a farthing from the spending.

"So, by determining that every sixpence should

stand to me, and to me alone, for sixpence three farthings, I saw my pile swelling and rising like the grain of mustard seed. You say you cannot comprehend how infinitesimal savings ever mount up to a million. I am certain I cannot. Yet they do; and if the farthings be not saved, the pounds, the hundreds, and the thousands, will not exert themselves to that end. The big things have to be convinced that a man is in grim earnest by seeing him take incredible pains with the little, before they try to puff themselves out. Mine were left in no doubt."

Bugbrooke had spoken with an effort, yet as if he were forced to make it, and could not stop himself. The old reminiscences were so eloquent to him that beads of perspiration stood on his forehead. But soon his aspect changed. He drew a deep sigh of relief as he resumed: "One Christmas Eve I had been sitting up late with my ledgers. I was not obliged to think of the next morning. Though I grudged Bank Holidays, and have spent many a quarter of an hour cursing the meddlesomeness of St. John Lubbock, they gave me a quiet time for making up my yearly accounts.

"The house was asleep betimes. It saved light and firing. No Christmas junketings for me. I had the latest Stock Exchange list before me to verify values. I booked the totals; so much for Insurance Shares, so much for Grand Trunks, so much for Red Leaf tin, so much for Great Northerns, so much for this, that, and the other. A column and a quarter; and the first £100,000 was reached. Column by column went by, and the hundreds of thousands sterling filed in. The total had come to £900,000, and a bare half column of figures remained to be added.

"'I must have known,' you say, 'what I was worth, without waiting for Christmas Eve to tell me.' May be yes, may be no. One may be in possession of all the premisses, with the conclusion lying enfolded within them, and not choose or dare to turn the brain's bull's-eye on, and look at it. I had not dared. I trembled — I can feel the quiver now — as my pen spitted the few remaining figures. All but — all but — and not! I turned back. Actually I had mistaken — or had I been playing at deceiving and tantalizing myself? — a £90,000 for a £70,000! Time, indeed, when I blundered like that, to leave off scraping. It was yes, yes, yes, — absolutely yes, with £10,000 to spare. I jotted down ' = £1,000,000'; and I sank back in my chair.

"True at last; I was a millionaire; and twelve

o'clock struck. Christmas Day had begun, and
the waits at the corner public-house burst into a
tumultuous carol. The bliss of that moment!
'You suppose it must be delightful to attain to the
dignity of a millionaire.' You do not appear to
understand what it signified to me. No more dis-
graceful drudgery. No grinding of poor men's
bones to make me bread, after a plentiful inter-
mixture of potato. No humiliating cheese-paring.
No timorous inquiry as to the law and the lee-
shore. No dirty little prudences. No reckoning
of odd shillings. No brazening of my face, and
steeling of my nerves. No more slynesses and
abject shynesses. No more acceptance of congratulations over sharpness which have been like
stings. Persons who have never had to condescend
to small profitable tricks in scrambling upwards
into wealth, talk as if they imagined that the doers
enjoyed them. They wish for an end, and have to
consent to the means which they may, quite consistently, abhor. I can see now that I always
loathed them, though I had to put a brave countenance on, and affect to think them commercially
laudable.

"Now you know why chiefly I am glad to be a
millionaire. It is respectable, and it allows one to
be respectable. There is an ascertained respecta-

bility in it which affords a sense of freedom such as I
never enjoyed before in the whole course of my life.
I no longer am afraid of amusements because they
might relax the nerves.   Greediness for money
does not sit upon me, a stifling nightmare.   On
that Christmas Eve I felt like a captain who dis-
covers himself inside a safe, still harbour, when, the
instant before, he imagined he was drifting on a
mangling reef.   I opened the window, and tossed
all the silver in my waistcoat pocket out to the
approaching music.

"I clapt to the ledgers with a bang, and went
off to bed.   Alas! there was nobody to wake, and
bid me a happy Christmas.   The poor wife — she
died when I dare say I had scarce a half million.
We could not afford for her to winter in the
Riviera, which might have cured her.   I slept, as
you will be surprised to hear — I was surprised
myself — as sound as a top.   When I opened
my eyes it was upon a new world.   As usual, I
had been called at six.   Usually I had jumped up
at once.   Now I cried out that I was to be called
again at eight, and should want some hot water.
I dressed slowly and comfortably.   My drudge of
a housekeeper was amazed at the good breakfast
I eat.   Instead, after breakfast, of pulling out my
accounts, I went to church.   There I meditated

on the life I was commencing, and was only sorry that there was no sermon.

"It was rather vexatious that I had ordered no orthodox Christmas dinner, not having foreseen how the total would turn out. I could not go and dine sumptuously at the inn. People do not go from home to dine at an hotel on Christmas Day, and I desired to do what people do. Still, I managed to be sociable in my own company, and in that of a bottle of old port. Boxing Day was an agreeable interregnum; for I needed a little contemplation of the changed prospect before I entered into possession. But the day after I went to my solicitor and agent. I instructed them to wind up all my wretched little businesses as quickly as they could. They were to sell the tenement houses, to compound liberally with my debtors, and generally to take care that no ghost of the bygone cozening money-spider should flit round the respectable me of the future.

"In time all was decorously settled. The ugly web, which it had required two-thirds of a life to weave, was broken up and floated away in a quarter of a year. I bought a house in Russell Square, where I shall be happy to see you whenever you are passing; and I studied how they live in the Square. I have a good house substantially furnished. Pictures honestly painted by real painters hang on the walls. Anybody can see them who passes by in the minutes dark enough for the blazing fire to light the room, and not dark enough for the blinds to be pulled down. I give dinners well cooked, with sound wine during them and after. I play a fair rubber, I subscribe to Mudie's, and read novels with a thirst of fancy accumulated in forty years of abstinence.

"I subscribe to all the parish charities. My system is to make an average of the total from the Square, and add ten per cent to my own pro-portional rate for arrears. I would gladly sub-scribe more, if the average rose, but I do not like to do anything uncommon. If I saw a sovereign lying in the street, nobody being near, I would not pick it up. I prefer to find I have ridden to the meeting-point of two fares, that with a whole con-science I may give the extra sixpence. I have schooled myself not to mind, though there has been a hole in my pocket, and half a crown has tumbled through — not that there often are holes now. I invite all my third cousin's children and grandchildren to Christmas dances. I remember the wedding days of friends, and send handsome souvenirs. Nobody can impute to me the absurd eccentricities of three-lettered beneficence. I should be ashamed to be caught playing pranks like that. But I do whatever other people do, only the least little better than they.

"Look at the way I dress. No one could accuse me of being more or less in the fashion than a hundred other members of this very club. The back of my great-coat has constantly been mistaken for one of a dozen other great-coat backs. I say to my tailor, 'Select any one of your other customers you please, of good fortune, with my cut and look. You need not tell me who he is. Dress me like him.' I am not afraid to tell my parson that I am well off, and that I shall subscribe with pleasure to his charities as much as he considers handsome.

"Nobody has ever heard me either say or deny that I am a millionaire. All that I wish to make clear to the world, including myself, is that I am not one of the money-grubbers. I stand and think of them, and look at them, from a distance, and I can thankfully declare I am not. I am safe out of the unclean riot, and cunning, and uproar, and cannot well remember when I might have been reckoned as part of it all. Only to think, that, if the fault in the Great Potassium Wheal had revealed itself a month before, instead of a month after, I climbed out, leaving my shares inside, I might still be shouting, and tumbling, and picking and next-door-to stealing, with the rest of the crew ! "

It was getting late, and we left the Club together. Bugbrooke hailed a cab, and invited me to ride, on my way home, as far as Russell Square. Manifestly there was a little struggle as we neared it. The old Adam incited him to accept my suggestion that we should go halves. But he recollected in time, and then seemed even pleased at the opportunity of putting his hand into his own pocket alone. I was relieved, too. Millionaires are rather fond of claiming half cab fares, and treating the extortion as a joke.

CHAPTER XIV.

THE HANDSOME LIVER.

IT was strange, but several weeks passed before I turned up another millionaire, after Bugbrooke's interesting disclosure of his true character. I walked the streets for hours together with both my eyes wide open, in vain. After all, a good many men in London wear burst boots and frayed shirt cuffs who are not millionaires. Besides, one cannot always manage to have a near view of the left side of the nose. Millionaires have unconsciously contracted a habit of turning that side away. On the other hand, happily, it is impossible to say where one will not light upon a specimen. I came on one lately in circumstances as unlikely as could possibly be imagined.

I was walking along a thoroughfare which I need not particularize. Narrow as it is, it contains many fine houses, some magnificent, overlooking a royal park. A heavy shower fell, and I stood up for shelter in the porch of one of the finest. After a minute or two, a gentleman hurried underneath it. A little girl held each

174

hand, and he was telling stories. "Stay a moment, father," I heard one of the two say; "you shan't ring till the good fairy has eaten the sugar nose." I saw that it must be the owner of the mansion.

As I had no right, either to occupy his doorstep or to hear his tale, without an invitation, I began to move away. "Pray do not go into the rain," a pleasant voice was saying, when it broke into an exclamation: "If it isn't Marmosette." So it was. They called me that at the Evangelical school at Clapham, from my second name, Marmion, and used to try to feed me with flies and slugs and spiders. Wat Wray was at school with me — his guardian was a sour Evangelical — and had been one of my tormenters. As invariably happens when two men meet on a doorstep, one apparently well-to-do, and the other not, both of us were surprised and delighted. Wat insisted that I should stop and lunch. He owed me that from old times. He rang, promising a conclusion of the fairy's adventures hereafter. The door was opened by a tall footman. Others in the hall took my coat and hat, and conducted me into a room to wash my hands. The whole place was an enchanted palace, full of flowers, statues, paintings, and china. Birds sang and gleamed in an exquisite aviary. A gigantic wolf-hound rubbed his head against me, and a chinchilla cat purred on the staircase about my muddy feet.

As I entered the drawing-room, Mrs. Wray, amiable, comely, and refined, advanced to greet me. Luncheon was announced, and did not belie the house. From the dining-room, Wray and I adjourned for coffee and cigarettes to his library. He inquired cordially, but delicately, what I was doing. I revealed to him — who, I saw, was not likely to pick my brains — my researches into the natural history of millionaires. He laughed, and said I was welcome to anatomize him, though he did not call himself a millionaire — he was only a Russia merchant. I laughed, too; for I have learnt to trace a millionaire, and Wray fulfilled none of the primary conditions. I could not perceive the millionaire wrinkle, though, to be sure, half his face was in shadow. He did not dress shabbily: not a button off, not a loose thread about neck-tie or collar. All the appointments were perfect. The servants were the exact number, neither too many nor too few. Nothing was lacking, and nothing was superfluous. Everything fitted like a glove. Each picture was charming to look at, and lent a grace to all the rest. Books were everywhere, nowhere in the way, and all readable. There was an air of wealth ever flowing, and never stagnating, in the manner it must to grow millionaires. So I resigned myself to a holiday, and to being comfortable, as it was too wet to go real millionaire-hunting that afternoon. I begged Wray at all events to explain what he had been doing since he entered life. Whether he were a positive millionaire or not, he had certainly, I said, succeeded in securing more comfort from money than most of the recognized millionaires whose acquaintance I had hitherto made.

"I left school, as you may recollect," he said, "to go to Oxford. When I had taken my double first there I volunteered to join my uncle Hucka-back at his office in Crutched Friars. I believe he had once been a Manchester warehouseman in a large way. But he was grown old and timid, and his business was dwindling. Every venture frightened him. Nobody could be more careful and self-denying. Yet it was all to no good. The world thought him rich, and I knew he was poor.

"After a couple of years of initiation into the alphabet of city trade, he called me into the par-lour one evening. 'Your ways and mine, Wat,' he said, 'do not agree, and I do not know that you are wrong. But if you be not, I must be; that's certain. So, off I go. I have enough to live on; and, as you are my heir, I make over to you from to-night as part of your inheritance my business here, for what it may be worth. I am heartily sorry it is not worth more. I have had conveyed into your name all the partnership plant and assets. When you have ruined the connection and yourself, you will find a knife and fork at the old place. I do not say you will ruin it, and I lay down no conditions. All the same, I hope you will keep on Grimsby. He has a head on his shoulders, though, if you be right, I have done my best to spoil the youngster.'

I thanked my uncle, and was installed in his place. Grimsby was my uncle's clerk, and some ten years my senior. He had been a workhouse apprentice, and had a wonderful head for figures. As my uncle had candidly avowed, he had spoilt him. If my uncle was a hedgehog, Grimsby was a tortoise. But he has always had a surprising scent for money, if only there be somebody to dig the badger out. An admirable worker, too, though past his prime now, poor old boy. I appreciated his merits no less fully than his defects, and I offered him a junior partnership. Not very eagerly he accepted it. He has always mistrusted me as an unstable sort of person. I used his in-

stinct and arithmetic, and I made my own strokes.
Without delay I changed the whole system. The
balance with which my uncle had started me I
pretty well exhausted in laying in new goods.
New customers streamed in from I know not
where. I made three hundred per cent on a vast
consignment by sea to Siberia. Within three
years the whole business was on an extended and
prosperous footing. But it would not interest you
to hear how many thousands we gained by boot-
laces in Turkestan, by baby linen in the Soudan,
or by nightcaps among the Esquimaux. The only
point really deserving remark in my career — not,
you must recollect, in Grimsby's — is that I have
constantly observed the maxim, which, when he
saw me practising it, so vexed my good old uncle:
'Spend while you make.' "

On its face such a principle, I could not conceal,
appeared to me audaciously contradictory to all
right doctrines of money-making. I have never
been acquainted with a millionaire's early life
which has not consisted of obedience to a rule
diametrically the contrary. No human beings can
be more extravagantly prodigal than those who
have attained millionaire rank. Before they have
arrived, their one axiom is that incomes are not
earned to be spent. Can any rule be more self-

evidently wise? I was sorry, therefore, to listen to Wray's paradox; for it confirmed my fear that he was not of millionaire stuff. However, I did not mind hearing him talk, and no cigars could be more prodigally admirable. I dissembled, therefore, my concern; and he proceeded to expound his method.

"Year by year," he said, "when I balance my books, I have divided my share of the profits into two portions. One I put to the capital account, and the other to income. My first clear total was £450, and I appropriated £150 for personal expenditure in the next twelvemonth. My uncle and Grimsby earnestly advised me to economize something out of the £150. I determined I would not, in spite of temptations to accumulate. I had to live carefully, for fear of running over the margin, and into debt; with the result that I had £7. 10 to spare at the end of December. I used it up in a dinner to four or five old college friends.

"In addition to board and lodging, I had already extracted some luxuries out of the £142. 10. There was the gallery at the Opera. There were pence for crossing-sweepers. There were postage stamps for hard cases in the police-courts, and in famine-stricken corners of Persia. There

was often some forgotten book or print, or
cracked china plate of a rare factory, to be
picked up very cheap. I could afford to take a
voyage from the Thames to Aberdeen for my holiday. In any case, there were the ducks to feed
on Sunday in St. James's Park, and the peacocks
in Kensington Gardens. I kept my friends, some
in mansions like this, who were glad to ask me to
formal dinners, after which I sang duets with the
daughters of the house. Some were of the out-at-
elbows kind, and as good company, to whom it
was my privilege to lend occasional half-crowns.
For a guinea to a lending library, I had the run
of all modern literature. The day's work over, I
was my own master as fully as when I was at
Oxford. I lighted my lamp. The housekeeper at
my chambers had made up a good fire. I made
my own tea and toast, as I still can, and better
than any servant. With a novel, I was happier
than any of your millionaires.

" Our trade expanded in a dozen different directions. Grimsby and I between us combined the
gifts of short sight and long sight. He infallibly
detected insolvency and fraud. I could feel, a
twelvemonth off, the rising breeze which was to
waft us to fortune. I suppose I have mercantile
imagination. I had faith in my partner's aver-

sions; and he, though he has never been able to understand, or thoroughly tolerate them, has never refused to profit by my visions.

"Not to weary you with business talk, at the close of the tenth year my divisible profit was £5000. I kept my pledge, and my personal expenditure in the following year was £1666. 13. 4. I must have found it harassing, you say, to go on continually raising the scale. Not the least. Only lay out your scheme of life on simple lines and a broad canvas, and the rest is all detail. It is as easy to spend £50,000 on yourself as £200, if you let your tastes develop naturally and healthily. My tours were to the Tyrol or Italy, not to Leith Hill. I dined in Pall Mall instead of Bishopsgate, and drank claret in place of stout. I sat in the pit stalls, and not in the pit. My clothes were made in Jermyn-street, and not Holborn. I bought etchings rather than prints after letters, and sometimes a study by David Cox. I gave a banknote, and not shillings, to a real charity, and subscribed to memorials of dead poets.

"I had always indulged pleasant daylight caprices. Now I indulged them in gold, and not in silver or bronze. Still I sat up novel-reading over tea and toast; only my vigils were passed in a study in Half-Moon-street, which was dressed

in books with Paris bindings, and in coloured
Oriental porcelain without a chip. Except that
he suffered visible pain at the thought of my dissolute extravagance, Grimsby's protests at my
waste on such baubles of doubled opportunities
for lucrative investments added a fresh zest to
my enjoyment of a freehanded outlay. With trib-
ulation as well as triumph, the poor fellow, who
never, I fear, had a sufficient meal unless I forced
him to dine with me, would assert that, out of his
inferior dividend, he put by every half-year more
than I.

"A few years later, the personal dividend, to
be spent, like the manna of the Israelites, and
not stored, was £14,750. I had a little curiosity
about its disposal; for I happened to marry in
the January. I wondered how marriage would
practically modify my system. No; there was no
difference. My bride was charmed when I communicated the arrangement to her. She had been
afraid that, like other business men of whom she
had read, I must grasp and hoard till an age
when she and I would have no heart or teeth to
enjoy. She admired the fixed scale of allowance
principle prodigiously. It was better, she said,
than even if we had been annuitants.

"You object that the plan works smoothly only

when each year is more prosperous than its prede-
cessor. The habit of growing larger and larger
wants is, you think, tyrannical; and we should
have been miserable, or have plunged into debt,
had the personal dividend shrunk. We tried, and
discovered that it is not so. A dozen years ago,
my branch of trade experienced a crisis. The ex-
pendible share fell to £750. There was nothing
more for wife, children, and me. It amazed even
ourselves to observe how cleverly the system
accommodated itself to the unusual circumstances.
We sold our house in Brook-street to a diamond
merchant. Pictures, old silver, china, jewellery,
and the rest fetched excellent prices and many
panegyrics on the vendor's taste, at Christie's.
The books we retained. We moved into a fascinating cottage at Muswell Hill. Out of the less
marketable but particularly interesting residue of
our collections, my wife created a morsel of fairyland. Once a month we went to the cheap seats
at some good theatre. Our friends flocked to
afternoon tea and tennis on Saturday and Sunday.
They and we agreed that we had stolen a bit from
Watteau. Almost with regret we had to admit
at last that prospects in the City were clearing,
and that our picnic must end."

I suggested that the credit of the firm might

have been endangered by the change in the style of living. "Not at all," said Wray; "I simply stated the cause, and of course I was not believed. Everybody asserted that I had taken at last to virtuous hoarding, like Grimsby, and applauded my prudence in trebling my fortune as my family doubled. The real surprise was when, with the upward turn, which goes on still, I had to migrate here. I do not think I need move again. The house promises to remain big enough for us; for I buy neither many new pictures, nor many new books. I am become rather exacting and scrupulous. It is not every Turner or Burne Jones which will tempt me. Indeed, I am apprehensive sometimes that I am not doing my duty as consistently by art now as formerly."

I assured him that the fear was absurd; that the doubt, on the contrary, with many eminent moralists and economists who glanced at the treasures of art in his cabinets and on his walls, would be whether he had not already gone to criminal lengths in spending a fortune on pictures and bric-a-brac.

"Yes," said he, "if I had spent a fortune on them; but I have spent no more at any time than their share, if that. Can it be denied that painters, bookbinders, living or dead artists in porcelain and faience, in brass and iron and silver, embroiderers, and engravers of gems, are entitled to a part of the yearly income of a civilized age? My view is that they have as much right as, not more than, graziers, glaziers, and grocers. It is a gross injustice to encourage a state of mental culture which produces a Millais, a Solon, a Benvenuto Cellini, now or formerly, and not maintain the men, and richly. They all, in their degrees, have an indefeasible title to participate in the spending of easy fortunes. I have done my best to mete out justice to them, and am only afraid of becoming indolent. Why should Jones, the green-grocer, have his full share, and not Fantin? Civilized society needs the one as much, at least, as the other, and Wilkie Collins and Tennyson more than either.

"I am a steward of my money, first of all for myself. I owe it to my own life to beautify that with it. Next, I am a trustee of it for everybody else who can prove he is wanted by the community. Necessarily I am judge; who else should be? It is a pity that my tastes are not absolutely true and catholic. But I am obliged to give where my tastes are satisfied, limited as these unluckily are. It is my misfortune, not my fault, that I cannot build an Italian palace, which would offer a chance to that worthy genius, Marbles, R.A. But then I hate Italian palaces. I know I ought to be able to commission Fussy, R.A., to paint the Guildhall Banquet for the instruction of future generations. But I cannot abide his work ; and my rule is to spend on what I like, and not on what I dislike. What other rule can I follow ? Mine has its defects and its injustices, as I have acknowledged. Still, my wife and children and I have hitherto managed to like a good many different things among us, and to like spending a good deal on them."

By way of a compromise between politeness to my host and old friend, and a protest against a theory of mercantile economy which must be fantastically wrong if the practice of authentic millionaires be right, I threw out the remark that it must be agreeable to feel one can spend largely. By this I meant to insinuate a gentle rebuke. That is, my conscience desired to put on record, without offensiveness to delinquents like the Wray family, its conviction that a solvent man should be content to know he has the ability to be profuse, and not be. Wray would not avail himself of the golden bridge of my courteous reticence. "That is the kind of thing," he said, "which Grimsby is constantly repeating. For us, we are

fond of the spending itself.   Is not that flagitious!
I am not sure that I have not found a gratification,
though I have heard the possibility questioned, in
having occasion to lend.   I know I have lent, and
have kept my friends, in spite of proverbs.   I hope
I am even overcoming the propensity to blush
when I meet the debtors."

That appeared to me an interesting fact, and I
will not say but that I had some curiosity to try
whether it could be true.   In other respects, also,
I have tested my schoolfellow's method; and I
must say that his account of it almost errs in
moderation.   Never have I known anything less
like a millionaire's fashion of action, especially
in respect of evenness of expenditure.   I have
never met a genuine millionaire, unless Wray be
one, who could be open-handed all through, any
more than I have ever conversed with a Colney
Hatch patient whose common sense had not one
wide leak in it.   The essence of a millionaire is
that he cannot for the life of him avoid cheese-
paring   somewhere.   His   cheese-parings   have
brought him his million; and its instinct is to
keep itself together by the same process.   He
may not himself like the tendency when he has
climbed up.   It is too strong for him.   Disguise
it as he may, with extraordinary pains, out it

will at odd moments. I have known one give £300 for flowers at a ball to celebrate his completion of the second million, and save five shillings on cut turnips over a doorway, where they could not be smelt at. One tumbled, and I happened to smell at it. A millionaire may wear diamond studs worth £2000, and eighteen-penny gloves, which give at the thumb before the evening is over. He will poison guests who, he is sure, have no palate, with petroleum champagne. He will spoil a new hat to save nine-pence by waiting for the omnibus in a shower instead of taking a cab.

That is not Wray's way. It never seems to enter his mind that a penny saved is a penny got. He is a spendthrift on £60,000 a year as he was at Clapham on sixpence a week. He travels everywhere first class, as a matter of honesty, he pretends, to the shareholders who have provided first-class carriages for his sort, though more commonly than not he rides second or third with an acquaintance, or because a carriage of that class happens to be nearest.

In another important respect also he is ludicrously unlike a true-bred millionaire. A correct millionaire, while he tortures his eyes with the flicker of a single wax end, after the company is gone, turns a whole chandler's shop loose in his drawing-rooms before guests who do not know him from Adam, but will talk of the splendour of his ball. He is scriptural, and does not hide his light under a bushel. Now Wray does exactly the reverse, to the pain of his sincerest friends. I have· known him, without his knowledge that I knew, leap into a quicksand of insolvency, and back on the solid rock with a virtual bankrupt in his strong arms, and off again before the wretch could understand how near financial death he had been, or who had saved him.

Altogether he is a nondescript: and my conscience pricks me for having ranked him with the regular members of the profession. It is a mere chance if he cut up for a bare £250,000 apiece among his four children — brought up, too, with every luxury! For myself, I shall not desert either him or them; but I hope it will always be understood that, though he may, after all, have a million, I do not account him a millionaire.

CHAPTER ·XV.

THE MONEY-GRUBBER.

I have continued to frequent Wray's house for the sake of auld lang syne, though I must confess I do not like his principles. I have been rewarded for my fidelity to friendship. Wray often alluded to his partner Grimsby. I had known about Mr. Grimsby for years. Since I took to my present historical vocation I had been longing to make his personal acquaintance. If ever a model millionaire existed, it must, I was sure, be he. I have marked with a large cross in my diary the happy day when I had the honour of seeing him in the flesh.

I had been passing the afternoon at Wray's house, staying, on one Saturday, from luncheon till tea. Several persons had dropped in. They were in the drawing-room, admiring a recent purchase, a Titian glowing almost indecently for an old master. It was of a kind ·which would nowise suit either Wix or Splotch. Wray, who had been out of the room, came back with a wizened, little old gentleman, in a cheap rather than shabby coat.

The rest of the company politely drew aside, with a slight air of suppressed curiosity. They were not at all of the millionaire type. They assumed, as I could perceive, that Wray was doing one of his eccentric kindnesses — impertinences, some might call them, to his regular guests — to some foundling of genius whom he had picked up. He never has the propriety to think of the feelings of other and respectable people, when he plunges among them a lettered or artistic tatterdemalion out of the gutter.

Up he led the newcomer to the tea-table. Mrs. Wray, with her eager, happy smile, greeted him in a manner to turn an old man young again. Addressing her elder little girl, she told her to put four large lumps of sugar in the cup, and to carry it carefully to " Mr. Grimsby." Actually and positively it was the great Grimsby. I had never detected him in the folds of his coat, which had manifestly been taken for his visit out of brown paper. I had not guessed it, though he had a button off his waistcoat, and endeavoured to hide it by passing his watch-chain through the vacant hole. Now I looked and understood whither Wray's wrinkle, if he have any right to one, may have escaped. Mr. Grimsby had two, one on each side ! I edged myself near him, plying him with cakes. All millionaires love cakes, when they have not to pay for them. I have known one eat ten twopenny cheese-cakes, at the expense of an aunt who had come up to draw her half-year's dividend of £150. Mr. Grimsby consumed all he decorously could, with two cups of sweet, strong tea, and then said he must go. He uttered a contemptuous and indignant snort as he passed the Titian on its easel, precisely as if his money had gone to buy it.

I happened to have said good-bye at the same time, a little to Wray's disappointment, or, at any rate, surprise. With some cause, he had thought I meant to be asked to stay to dinner. As Mr. Grimsby was putting on his overcoat, I was in the hall. I am a sharp observer, and I had noticed that fortunately he was walking lamely. I said to him, "I am not aware, Mr. Grimsby"— "That's my name; how did you learn it?" he interjected, grumpily — "whether you be going my way, and would allow me to drop you any-where in my four-wheeler." I referred to a four-wheeler, which always gives me bone-ache, for I was sure that he detested Hansoms. "I do not think," he muttered, after a while, with a scornful glance at my bright boots, "that you are very likely to be going my way." "Myddelton Square is my destination," I said, with a brilliant inspiration. I knew Mr. Grimsby lived in Amwell-street, and I just remembered that my watch-maker's Private Chronometer Hospital was in Myddelton Square. My invalid watch was at the moment undergoing a cure there. "Much obliged," said he, "as it will not cost you a penny more. A shame to waste half a fare."

I had a four-wheeler hailed, deposited Mr. Grimsby paternally in it, and seated myself humbly opposite. He lolled on the musty cushions as luxuriously as if he were in a duke's barouche. His normal carriage is a 'bus, bussy. "The address?" asked I, though I knew it as well as if there had been a china plate and inscription over the dining-room window, as there would be if London recognized its greatest men. He named the number in Amwell-street, and there I left him. I may have been disappointed that he did not ask me in; but it was the thin end of the wedge. I do things plausibly even when nobody is looking behind. Accordingly, I called in Myddelton Square with an inquiry which really, in some conceivable circumstances, I might have wanted to make, though it happens I then did not.

As I came down the doorstep Grimsby was by the railings. It would have been a lucky coincidence, if it had been a coincidence. He saw I really had business in Myddelton Square, and had not invented a story — millionaires are suspicious — to track him home. But he was not there by chance. He had something of mine at home, and had followed me to the place where I said I was going, in order to be rid of it. In the hurry of descending before the thought could arise that he should share the cab fare, he had exchanged umbrellas. Thus, in place of his characteristic gingham he was saddled with a silk one, and a silver nameplate, or it might not have mattered. "Step in round the corner," said he, "and you shall have your goods. I don't care for stolen property, particularly when it is earmarked." I attended him to Amwell-street. He opened a mean door with an elaborate latch-key. "Can't be bothered," he said, "with servants in the house. Mine comes to tidy up in the morning, and leaves in the afternoon before I come home." The oil cloth of the hall was littered with letters, half-dividend warrants; the rest, County Court summonses. He showed me these with a sneer. They were for small amounts from ground-down tradesmen. "My principle," he said. "How can I tell else if they want their money?"

He took me upstairs to a room on the second floor, where a table was laid as if for an austerely earnest tea. "I shall have my supper," he said; "but I dare say you are going to your club. Every jackanape has a club now." I assured him I had no engagement, and that I liked nothing so much as a tea-dinner. "Just as you please," was his hospitable invitation. "Go away, or sit down and have supper; only, for goodness' sake, let me have mine." I sat down, and he had it.

Soon the coffee essence rose into his head, and he began to talk. That was a treat — to hear the illustrious Mr. Grimsby talk! Real working millionaire talk; none of your holiday, out-of-harness, spending talk, but getting talk! After the fashion of men who live much alone, and are compulsorily silent, he used to the full the rare opportunity of an audience. Nothing could have satisfied me better. I sucked the whole in. As soon as I was at home I wrote it down as I recollected it. Probably it may read interjectional, spasmodic, occasionally inconsequent. Repetitions will be found, surface contradictions, inconsistencies. A money-grubber's life — and his genius too — is rather a mixed mine. But it will be the student's fault, not that of Mr. Grimsby, or of S. M. Twygge, if he do not discover grains of gold everywhere.

Naturally he ·began by abusing his ·partner.

"There's a man for you! You are his friend,
aren't you? So am I. That's why I speak my
mind about him. I am rich enough at least to
be blunt and honest. He and I started with
everything on his side. His uncle, old Hucka-
back, gave him the business for nothing, and died
two years after, leaving him — the foolish old fellow — £10,000, if a penny, though he knew he
was encouraging a spendthrift. Nobody ever left
me anything. All I had was my apprenticeship.
When Huckaback made all over to Wray, Wray
offered me a partnership. To prevent the concern
from going to the dogs, I accepted. Yes; it may
have turned out a good thing for me. It certainly
has for him. No; I do not deny he has some
business capacity. He jumps to conclusions fast,
and, well, yes, on the whole, safely. But, for
steady plodding, compare him and me! Compare
the Crystal Palace fountains and the handle of
a dry pump! Why, sir, I remember, one Friday,
as I was coming into the office, a fellow from
Hackney was going out. I looked him all over.
I went to the desk. They were booking a consignment of fifty pounds' worth of calicos to him,
by Wray's order. 'Wait,' I said, 'till Tuesday.'
He broke, Sir, on the Monday, and we saved the
money!"

I took occasion to mention that at Clapham
I too had taken a prize above Wray, when he
did not compete, for the best essay on the number
of times shekels are named in the Book of Judges.

"I have no confidence," proceeded Mr. Grimsby,
"in the man." "In the Hackney man?" I
asked. "No; none in Wray. Here one minute
and gone the next. Jumps about like a bird on a
bush. He has luck, and that has made it worth
my while to keep in with him — and I pity his
poor children. But no seriousness; no decorum.
I don't mean in business hours. Anybody can
be vigilant and grasping then. But look at him
when the office is closing. Off my fine gentleman
flies to a picture gallery, or to lawn-tennis, and at
his age! He is not ashamed to drive from the
counting-house door, calling out before the clerks,
'the Row!' 'Christie's!' or some such reckless
place where money is spent, and not earned.

"He does not blush to avow that he is fond of
spending. Says he has a right to spend out of
his abundance. What difference can that make?
A shilling is as much a shilling, though it have
twenty million companions, as if it have none.
It is a mere accident that it is in Wray's or my
pocket. It might be in yours. Anybody with
a conscience will first think what it, not what

he, its temporary guardian, wishes to have done with it. Do you suppose it wants to be squandered on a cab, when the man can walk? Wray will not save, he declares, more than what he terms the fixed allowance. As if there could be a fixed limit to saving! If he were a pauper, I could understand his spending; but comfortably off, and not to go on!

" You thought, you say, he was not so well off. No more is he. What's a million, more or less, except a nest-egg to addle — hatch, I mean — more millions on? My way has always been, and I suppose I know" — " No man better," I remarked civilly. " What can you tell about it?" said he testily; "but no matter; my way, whether you approve it or not, is to have ragged ends. Nothing like a ragged end to save on to. I invariably buy something and a fraction. Buy £20,000 of Midland stock. There it is and will be. Buy £20,753. I warrant you, that holding will never rest easy till it be £30,000. You will be a fool if you let it sit down there, and do not make it fret off to £30,219. Round sums are fascinating, from a distance. Always be trying to perch upon them, and always contrive to hop an inch further.

" What do I judge enough to stand at? That's the common craze. People go on talking of a million, two millions, three, as if, when they had it or them, they had nothing to do but fold their arms, and see the pile dropping to bits. Nobody ever yet made his million, and stuck there; no Englishman, that is. I have heard of an American who tried it, and he ought to have been locked up. There is no finality, as newspaper men in their jargon call it, about a million. That is its beauty. It leads you on. It insists upon companionship."

I ventured to remark that the difficulty in the practical operation of the principle which occurred to me was, that, according to it, no millionaire can feel that he has an income to live on. The income never, as it were, becomes income, and remains only capital, which goes rolling on. I entirely concurred in the condemnation of Wray, who has all his life long been eating up half of what, till his million was made, morally was capital. Nevertheless I should have supposed a full-grown millionaire had a right to close his capital account, and treat the yearly proceeds as money to be enjoyed, while he turned his hand to charitable occupations.

The theory I had innocently enunciated was more repulsive to Mr. Grimsby than Wray's practice. "Live on my income, my competence, my comfortable income, as it appears to you!

Devote my energies to the service of the public!" he cried out. "But do you not see that I am labouring for the world in the noblest manner while I husband my investments? Is the ox to be muzzled that treads out the corn! Is he to be told to go to his manger and feed there? Am I to squander my hard-earned store, which you choose to ticket as income, upon my own keep? That is sheer extortion. I am worth my salt to the world, and the world must maintain me."

I sought to allay his not unreasonable anger at a demand which he construed as brought against him in the interest of a greedy, niggardly public, by assuring him I had been thinking of his convenience alone. From my experience of the habits of other millionaires I had inferred that they claimed the right, on their own accounts, to leisure for philanthropy. When they emerge from their several chimneys as millionaires, and wave their sweeps' brushes triumphantly at the top, I have found that they commonly take to philanthropy as a vocation. I had presumed, therefore, they felt they were getting something by it, as notoriously nobody else is a gainer. I merely thought Mr. Grimsby was as much entitled to his share of the advantage, whatever it may be, as any of his brethren.

"Who," he exclaimed, "do you imagine is more of a philanthropist than I ? What is truer philanthropy than the cultivation of the art of growing richer and richer ? Money comes running to me like a chicken to its mother in the hen-coop, because it feels it is safe with me for good works. Who watches against its misuse so diligently? Who applies it to such profitable purpose ? It is torture to me to have a grain of it wasted without an abundant return. When I have a few spare pounds, I sit with my books open a whole evening before I can decide how to employ them. There's true charity for you; true thoughtfulness for the welfare of the working classes.

"It is not, as you may suppose, only able-bodied investments which I befriend. Many is the sturdy cripple, limping for lack of a temporary crutch, which I have set on its feet for good and all. I tell you I have felt all aglow with humanitarianism, if that be your word for it, on buying up a most promising, a most beneficial, concern, bound to thrive after it has sown its wild oats, and ruined three several proprietaries. I have meditated on the trustful widows, the guileless country clergy, the brave half-pay officers, who had hoped for ten per cent, and lost both dividends and principal. I am not the man to let all their sacrifices and privations, a most admirable foundation, go for nothing.

"My first duty is to my money, to secure that it has all its powers thoroughly and permanently exerted. The greatest philanthropist is he who makes eight per cent grow, where two per cent grew before. There is no surer proof of the fulfilment of the obligations of wealth, than a manifest propensity in it to yield larger and larger returns, and to become more and more. I have heard myself called money-grubber in the open street, and by a man who declined to take up an allotment of new stock in the Gasometrelectric Power Company, because he alleged he wanted the cash to build a wing to the Cataleptic Hospital, run by a rogue of a secretary and a troop of medical vultures. With the premiums I pocketed in due course from the Power Company and similar adventures, I am nourishing honest, working families all over the world. Sailors on every ocean are living on my savings. Trappers at Baffin's Bay owe their pemmican to me. Without me there would be tears, sulks, and thinness in the Sultan's harem. I contributed the final cantilever to the Forth Bridge. I am suppressing dacoity in Burmah, and am growing spices in Borneo. When I read in the newspaper praises of directors, engi-

neers, and architects, I often laugh to myself.
Think I, ' all to the glory of Smith and Jones, and
not a word of Grimsby? Yet they would have
been in a fine hole but for my advances, and my
generous confidence in their ability to yield them
their proper return.'

" ' Am I annoyed,' you ask, ' at the parable of
Dives?' Not in the least. Do I look like Dives?
Could not I almost go through the eye of a needle?
I am satisfied that I do my duty, and not in purple
and fine linen. I lead none of your easy lives.
Up early and to bed late, and all hard work between. Not so much the business; though I keep
a sharp eye on the balances. I let Wray and the
clerks do most of the routine now. My time is
too valuable, and I have done my share already.
My own investments are occupation enough.

" I have to survey the whole field. One investment has to be matched with another, rich present
profits in this to be measured against a more magnificent future in that. Though I generally stick
to the solidity which is, and help it to grow more
solid, and have no liking for propping up incura-
bles from my wood-stack, there are, as I have told
you, exceptions. I have to look narrowly that I
do not warn disguised angels off my strong box.
The worst trouble is only commencing when I

have chosen. I have to study accounts, present and past. I compile biographies of secretaries, actuaries, managers, and directors. I must sit through meetings, and heckle the chairman. I am not one of your investors who squabble over an Atchison, Topeka, and Santa Fé scheme, and have not been at the pains to learn where Topeka is. As I look back over fifty years of scraping, and scrambling, and squeezing, I can see that nothing but a high sense of duty can have borne me up and spurred me onwards.

"Duty, that is the millionaire's keynote and keystone. There is no sounder teacher of morals than money. At any rate, I never sat under a better preacher. Look at us millionaires. We are not witty, or handsome, or wise, or eloquent; but show me a class more sober, temperate, law-abiding, self-denying. We do not steal, when we have our million. We do not elope with our neighbours' wives. We do not brawl. We do not sell our party for the mess of pottage of a colonial governorship. Who ever heard of a millionaire beating his wife, or, in the country, not going to the family pew? I could myself, at any time, pauperize a whole parish with almsgiving, if I chose; and I don't choose. I could trade in the rescue of ragged genius from despair, and bank

clouds of wives' and children's blessings for Job
Grimsby. Could I not, if I would, be a soft silly
like Wray, and with more to back it? Men like
me have power, unlimited power, to do mischief,
if we were not so conscientious. No power like
that of gold. It raises armies, and storms citadels.
Its dearth saps the loyalty of nations. Its plenty
knits fealty beyond the force of tyranny and folly
to loosen. You ask, 'How about happiness?' Do
not heed what philosophers babble of the impo-
tence of gold to give it. Gold, if there be enough,
can give it; at all events, everything from which
it comes. It can buy beauty. It can buy amiable
looks and words. It can insure health generally,
and German waters always. Friendship, they say,
is independent of it. Is it? Where are pleasanter guests to be met than round the rich man's
table? He may be the dullest of oafs. Poets,
story-tellers, jesters, dignified yet benevolent clergy,
legal sages, and good fellows will not disdain his
hospitality. Money, a heap of money, is bottled
industry. It is bottled space and time. It is bottled pleasure. It is the one unfailing dynamo and
accumulator. It is bottled sunshine.

"A millionaire has but to determine what he
will do, or let alone. As he sits by himself he
can coin his money into any shape he, that

is to say, his conscience, pleases. It may be a seat in Parliament. It may be a restored cathedral. It might be a baronetcy. It may be racers and gold cups. It may be husbands for his unprepossessing, elderly daughters. Very malleable is gold. The world is for the rich, the really rich, to carve as they will ; and the best of it is they can, if they please, like me, never carve it at all. They may eat their cake, in dreams, and keep it safe in the cupboard all the while.

"I have read somewhere that you cannot carry your pelf, and lands, and shares with you. Cannot you, though ! Any millionaire who has a conscience, and takes the trouble, will hold fast his substance, deep as his executors shall bury him. He can speak from the grave so loudly that posterity will have to listen. Whenever I dive below I promise you I shall go under with a splash which will echo long around. Life ends ; gold lasts ; gold does not rust. The emptiest money-bubble never wholly bursts. Mississippi bonds colour and float, if you are patient with them, and have bought cheap.

"Not that I go in much for bubble-blowing, except for a game. I like ringing metal, and every coin, as it passes my fingers, has, I warrant, an imprint of me left upon it. The title of stocks I have held will have to be traced through me. I am a link in their existence as they are in mine. I should like to see them affecting to forget their master because he is dead! They will not try. They feel how much they owe me. I drew them from obscurity. I delivered them from the whims of idle spendthrifts. I nursed them from weakness to health. They know that I am all theirs, and they are loving and pitiful.

"They like it, as I like it, on a dreary, drizzling, November Sunday afternoon, when the bells are jangling, church and muffins, and I unroll them, my list of stocks and securities, and we add up totals together. I go back then into the past, and am content with the present. Sweetheart I never had before my first £100 of London and North Western. I recollect how I courted that as rarely human mistress has been wooed. It has paid me back kiss for kiss. It is not jealous though I have other sweethearts now besides. I was solitary once. None ever made friends with me. I am no longer companionless and friendless. As I call, my investments, shares, and dividend warrants come forth in flocks to answer. Puny, withered, little animal as I am, — and I know it, — they would nearly persuade me I am lovely. They believe in me. They do not snarl and snigger ' Miser.'

Round my chair they hover, and tell strange stories how I won them, or they won me. They vow never to part, and entreat me, who am tender-hearted, not to desert them. How softly they beam upon me! How warm and velvety their lips! Hundreds of times they have cooed me to sleep, and turned Pentonville into Fairyland.

"But mind; there must be enough of them, or there must be the assured promise of enough. Money, to be of use, has to be sufficient to make a profession of it. None of your niggling competences for me. Let me bathe in gold, shovel it up by bushels, be able to dip my arms deep in the midst of it; or give me a stone-picker's wages, and have done with it!"

The illustrious, the truly venerable, man had by this time half forgotten my presence. He just recognized it so far as to be aware that it might not be prudent to expose his ledgers to a stranger, and compare his investments for the current week with the last. But his eyes dwelt with evident craving on the doors which separated him and them. I should have dearly loved to stay and study them with him, but that would have been indiscreet; and discretion is my forte. So I rose quietly, murmured a good-night, took my hat and umbrella, and quitted the room. As I descended the stairs I heard a cupboard unlocking, and knew Mr. Grimsby was about to be happy with his entries.   To think that Wat Wray should for half a lifetime have had such a pattern — an ideal pattern, a beautiful, heroic example — close by him, and go on muddling away his money on himself!

CHAPTER XVI.

ENJOYMENT OF A MILLION BY PROXY.

YESTERDAY, as I was walking along Tottenham-Court Road — a charming place for a saunter, so elegant, so picturesquely gay — at the upper end I stumbled, in a brown study, against Mr. Grimsby. We have become tolerably intimate; for I am often at Wray's, and so is he. We have formed a habit of walking away together after tea, and comparing notes on our poor friend's infatuation in spending when he ought to save.

"Only think," said Mr. Grimsby, continuing his comments of the Saturday before, "his bits of sticks, shares, and things have to be divided among four children. Bare pittances! A father with a heart in him would be pinching and piling, to put them as comfortably before the world as himself. They have not a chance, as it is, of very much more than £10,000 a year apiece." I suggested that, with their bringing up, they would probably make ducks and drakes of that or more, if any windfall from a compassionate friend came to them. He did not seem to attend to me, as

211

he went on: "The man, Sir, ought to live on a thousand himself. He might then hope to save a tolerable sufficiency for his destitute orphans. Now, there is Hempson, whom I have to see this morning. Something like family affection, his. One grandchild; and he means the young fellow shall be as well off as he."

At the moment we were opposite St. Giles's Church. Mr. Grimsby never carries a watch; had one once, a legacy, and sold it. "Plenty of clocks in London," he says, "without £11. 10 ticking themselves into dust." He looked up. "Bless my soul!" he exclaimed; "five to twelve, and the haunted side of Berkeley Square to be knocked down cheap at the Auction Mart at the half-hour!" I told him there was plenty of time; a cab would do it in twenty minutes. "Nonsense," said he. "I haven't ridden in a cab since you took me, four months back, and paid. You are not going city-wards this morning, I suppose? The 'bus for me, and that's half an hour. I see you have nothing to do. You may as well carry this letter for me. Nothing valuable, convertibly valuable, inside, or I would not ask you. It is for my friend — well, not exactly a friend — Hempson, in Goodge-street. You can take a receipt, and post it me. I'll settle for the stamp when we meet at

Wray's in the autumn." He thrust into my hands a heavy, brown paper parcel, with a clammy smell of vellum, hailed a Bank omnibus, into which he painfully climbed, and sat down on a basket of clothes going to the wash.

I cannot say that I like being enlisted as errand-boy with less than no pay; but I could not help myself, and there was the admired Hempson to be pumped. I walked back down Tottenham-Court Road to the address in Goodge-street. If I were a millionaire, I think I scarcely should select Goodge-street for my town residence. Still, I admit that it is central; and to live in a private house in Goodge-street is rather distinguished.

I rang, and, after surveying me in a manner to be able to identify me in a row of pickpockets at Marlborough-street, the slattern who answered the bell showed me into the parlour. There sat an old man, much older than Grimsby, with the *ruga sestertiensis* and all complete. He opened the parcel, examined its contents, tried, with a grunt of disapproval, the quality of the string and wrapper, and wrote out a receipt. As he was about to bid me good-morning, fortunately I recollected the famous meeting at Cannon-street of Estremadura proprietors, when Mr. Hempson declared himself the largest holder, and bearded the board. Estremaduras, I had seen in the second editions, were up, and I told him. He chuckled, and had enough gratitude after that to say I might take a chair.

As I could not tell how long I should occupy it, I plunged right out with my two habitual questions, how he made his million, and what he did with it? If one is to be kicked out, better be kicked out with the gloss upon one's impertinence than after the waste of precious time in beating about the bush. Rather to my surprise, he did not resent my inquisitiveness, and seemed pleased to be interrogated. As usual, however, he passed by the first question as a conventionalism, like "How do you do?" "Breeches," he ejaculated, gruffly; and then he seriously began.

Now it happened that I knew something about him. After he had turned his million, he started, I was aware, with a fit of riotousness. I mentioned the fact to him. "It is perfectly true," he said. "I had always thought, as I was measuring young sporting earls for their hunting breeches, or exchanging their bills for my cheques, how I should like to have my fling also. For thirty-five years I had envied them, and meditated on the pace I would go whenever my pile was made. At last I discovered one day that it was all right. Young Cleggshaye, whose contingent reversion I had bought seven years before for £12,000, broke his neck jumping down a well staircase, which he took, after supper, for the front doorstep.   His elder brother, whom likewise I had accommodated, went off a half a year before in a fit of tipsy apoplexy.   His father was drowned yachting in Norway, and his grandfather died of a mayonnaise.

"The last three melancholy events were all pulled off in a week.   Together the four deaths, though not a Cleggshaye had paid for his breeches in twenty years, stood me in the odd £250,000 which I needed to finish my million.   I had nothing to do but sell the breeches business to a limited company, which is now wound up, and to sit down, not in Goodge-street, to enjoy life.

"Bah! it tasted bitter in the mouth.   I raced, under another name, and I gambled.   I drank, and I did all the rest of it that gentlemen do.   It was of no use; I was always reckoning the cost. I subsided, unconsciously, into the habit of lending money to old customers, and taking good care of the security.   Nobody could see in me anything but Breeches, attending conveniently in the ring for a job of bill-discounting.   The worst was, I could never see anything different in myself.   One cannot learn of a sudden to scatter and enjoy, when one has been on a tailor's board, or a high

stool, for thirty or forty years. A man has to be
bred to it as to a profession, and I had been bred
to skinflinting.

"At length I said to myself: 'Hempson, Hempson, you will end in Hanwell if you do not
beware. Money-grubbing is your fate. No good
fighting against it.' An impudent young rascal,
the last man to whom I should have dreamt of
applying for advice, completed my cure. 'Get
drunk,' he said, 'Breeches, on champagne, and
have your photograph taken.' I had it done, and
Moses, the sight I was! I thought I had been a
bluff, rough, frank sportsman; here was I; grim,
sly, sneaking, cringing, and all the while as tipsy
as the best of them!

"That was the end. I woke up as sober as a
Judge — if that's saying much — though my hand
shook so I could not shave. I was happy and
cheerful, nevertheless. I had seen a vision. You
must know I have had a wife. Dead? Yes; but,
first, off with an actor. Then it was that I took
heavily to money-making. An opiate that, at least.
But she left me the girl, a good-looking, self-willed
wench. At times she lived with me, but generally with her aunt. My wife had been a music-
hall singer, and my girl's aunt was a Particular
Baptist. So at sixteen Susan Esmeralda was sick

of hymns, and married a colour-sergeant, — Elliott, he called himself. It did not matter much :
Ashantee ended him, and she died of her first and
only child, a boy. I had never seen her since the
week before she was married, at a Registry Office,
till I bade her good-bye in her pauper's coffin.

"Her baby was in his cradle near. I could not
be troubled with him, and I handed him over to
his great-aunt, to bring up as successfully as she
had his mother. I paid for his education in a moderate, simple sort. I never pretended to be very
affectionate to him, and I do not know why I
should have been. Even when I had made my
million I did not change. Necessarily he must in-
herit — I saw that. You do not suppose I was
going to be such an idiot as to throw away my
savings in charity-mongering. But I must confess
I had regarded his right of succession as a rather
disagreeable necessity. All of a sudden, when I
discovered that I could not enjoy my money myself, the boy occurred to me. There my chance
was. He had vagabond blood in him on both sides.
At the commercial school, to which I had sent him,
the masters reported they could make nothing of
him. His great-aunt declared him a castaway.
He was the heir to a million, and I resolved he
should be trained to play with it nobly in my
stead.

"I removed him straightway to the most expensive preparatory school I could find. Thence he went to Eton, to make friends of the right kind for a fellow to whom money will be no object. After Eton, a military tutor. Next, the Militia; and now, after a few tries, the Guards, I hope. There has never been any occasion to connect him with Joe Hempson, the breeches-maker. He is lawfully Henry Ralph Elliott, and I am his father's executor, or might have been, if his father the colour-sergeant had possessed anything to bequeath, and had made a will. No one need be inquisitive, and go behind a fair working name, not too fine and not vulgar, like Henry Ralph Elliott.

"The young gentleman steals in to see me when the supplies are low. Consequently, I see him pretty often, and I screw out of him all he has been up to. That is life; and for me, too! He belongs to his West-End clubs already. He keeps horses, my horses, at Melton and at Newmarket. I pay for Sunday dinners at Richmond. He goes for me behind the scenes at the theatre. Sometimes I walk behind the chairs in the Row to watch him riding past. He knows everybody; bows to the smartest lady; nods to the most notorious man. All by my guineas; and I go home, and out with my books, where are my Lords and my Ladies, or their brothers, husbands, protectors, and fathers, contributing to make a good round property rounder for Joe Hempson's grandchild. He does not understand me himself one whit. I have seen him quake when he has brought a long account to be settled. Now and then I have offered to get a bill done for him if he can have it backed. I calculate how much I shall be making out of him and his fine friends. That's my little joke with him, though I do not tell him.

"That muddle-headed curmudgeon, Grimsby, chatters of the power of money, as if he knew. He locks it up in his strong-box, and fancies he is enjoying it because he might enjoy it. My money is not potential; it is actual. My way I call really using it. No sham about that."

I protested silently, which I find the most effectual way with wrongheaded millionaires, against the extraordinary misrepresentation of Mr. Grimsby's character; but I listened with interest to Mr. Hempson's development of his own somewhat peculiar system, as he proceeded: "All the dowagers in Belgravia are hunting me, though they speak of Henry Ralph, for their handsomest daughters. When I settle down, — that is, he, — I shall build a palace in Park Lane, and buy a castle in Northumberland. I — that is, he — may

become an art patron, and dine on a May Saturday at Burlington House. We may order a mon-
ster telescope, and keep an astronomer to discover
new planets, and christen them after us.

"Meanwhile he — that is, I — is the cleverest,
most fascinating, most brilliant, figure in Club-
land. They cheer me when he enters his box at
the Opera. I am played and danced at, and sung
to. He — that is, I — is not virtuous; no, not at
all; yet there is not a charity in London which
would not welcome him on its council. Extravagant, Henry Ralph has been called, and a dissolute
prodigal. Very likely, and why not? He shall
have enough to last his time; and in truth, if it
be all the same to him, I should be better pleased
than not for that I have saved to last no longer.
I have saved it for one; I have no concern with
an indefinite number of great and great-great-
grandchildren.

"'It will soon go,' you say? Not so very soon.
I have done my sums, and know better. The turf,
with a little plunging — I have so many scores of
thousands ready for that. For it I boiled down
last year young Singleton's Worcestershire estate.
So much for meaning to break the bank at Monte
Carlo. Here it is. Reckon the cantatrice at
£20,000, and two-thirds as much for the ballet

dancer. I have honestly put by for each. Here are the sums posted in the ledger; and I cannot believe there is a folly or a gentleman's vice which has not in my accounts its reasonable cash prepared to balance it.

"But I expect a visitor who has a right to be particular about the company he meets. I must wish you good-day."

As I let myself out, I encountered on the door-step an overdressed young man, a handsome, un-derbred, unwholesome cub, pallid, swollen, flabby, and insolent. He had just jumped off a dog-cart, with a big cheroot in his mouth. "One of the fat flies," said I to myself, "blundering into the web to furnish lucky Master Elliott's vicarious larder." In he swaggered past me, as if I had been the housemaid to open the door for his Highness. He slammed it on me, and I asked his tiger the name. "Captain Elliott," was the reply. "So ho!" said I to myself; "an agree-able, graceful toy, that, to buy and nurse and work for, and play with, and dream about!"

CHAPTER XVII.

THE MILLIONAIRE RELIEF AGENCY.

SOME time back I mentioned that I found the supply of public-spirited millionaires comparatively short. It seems long since I had occasion to relate a conversation with one of the type. I do not even now know whether Mr. Robert Ditchling ought more strictly to be classed with the public or with the private division of the order, with the Anarchists, if such a term could ever be used in connection with a million sterling, or with the Individualists.

I owed my original acquaintance with him, as that of old with Mr. Nathaniel Griggs, to Mr. Barstrow, "Charity-Wrecker Jeremiah." Mr. Barstrow is like the King of France, who nibbled fried pork cutlets between the courses at dinner. When there is no institution handy for breaking up, he takes a turn at depauperizing family life. The other day I met him, in a hurry as usual, in the Minories, with a companion sticking to him. "Can't wait," he cried; "have just heard of the most heart-rending case. A fine young man starting in life as a tripe seller; famous business; only wanting to be pushed; and he was an enthusiast; has printed a book with diagrams of the difference between tripe double and tripe single. Then an American tenth cousin, in oil, goes and dies. Tripe found to be next of kin. Will have the dollars; that is, ruin, drink, vagabondage. But I think I have unearthed a ninth cousin at New Tipperary. If so, he is saved. Conference now on in Charterhouse Square. You and Ditchling here should know one another. Good-bye."

On the strength of this informal introduction Mr. Ditchling walked with me as far as Aldersgate-street. But his talk was not amusing, and, as I did not know the figure he stood at, I was obliged to have business at the Dead Letter Department of the General Post Office.

Yesterday, however, I came across him again in very curious circumstances. Walking in the evening through Grosvenor Square, I recognized a face, or, I might say, a hat, stooping from under the area-gate of a well-known millionaire. It was Mr. Ditchling. My first thought, I confess, was that Mr. Barstrow had been playing off a practical joke upon me. Still, I am always sensible that it is trifling with edged tools to run the risk of cutting the most remotely possible millionaire. Accordingly, I bowed and addressed him by name. "Ah!" he said; "a friend, I believe, of Barstrow's?" "The same," I replied. "But permit me, I beg, to relieve you;" for he is old, and looked fagged, and was carrying a large old carpet-bag. The heaviest and mouldiest carpet-bags of millionaires are never heavy and shabby to me. They have a buoyancy and a flavour all their own.

He thanked me with a sigh, as, after a polite little struggle, he relinquished the bag to my keeping, "though," said he, "it is lighter now than it was this morning." I assured him my way was his; I was merely out for a stroll; and we walked on in company. Having discovered somebody to carry his abominable pack, he was in no hurry to resume it, and he placidly sauntered by my side. He halted before a respectably commonplace house in a long dull street off the Edgeware Road.—There are many long streets off the Edgeware Road, and none of them can be described as extremely lively.—He had hardly an option but to invite me in, and I accepted without enthusiasm or hesitation. Ushering me into the usual mausoleum of a self-respecting dining-room, he alluded to a cup of tea after my walk. I thought I might as well have the tea, which I had well earned, in any case; but, as I glanced at the old fellow's face in repose, I saw I had my millionaire into the bargain. Mr. Ditchling had the moneyed wrinkle admirably developed. I was resolved to extract his story.

I told him I could perceive that he was a millionaire, and I inquired, in my best candid way, how he had become one. "By slops mostly," he as simply answered; "and the rest, as far as I can remember, by picking the pearl oysters out of Persian Gulf sponges." He yawned slightly, as if the recollection were a nuisance, and proceeded: "But all that's plain sailing — not worth the talking of; only, young man, do not try at the wrong end. If you be studying with a view to a million, first determine what you are going to do with it. The misery I have witnessed through men amassing their millions, and not having learnt to spend them! This very evening such a scene! Ah! if people could understand all they lay themselves out for when they go into the millionaire line!"

He showed emotion, and I might not have ventured to interrupt his sad reverie, but he did it himself. As he lifted his head from his clasped hands, his eyes fell on the carpet-bag. "You found my old friend heavy," he said; "but you should have felt the weight when I carried it out at the beginning of the day." My curiosity now was fairly aroused, though, as you may imagine, I am by no means a prying person. I put a few leading questions, and he was not at all diffident in answering them. " You saw me," he said, " as I was leaving my friend Plowsy — " " By the area steps," I mildly interpolated. " By the area steps," he repeated, not appearing to suspect that the kind of exit called for explanation. " Now," he added, " I will tell you about poor Plowsy's case, and I trust it will be a warning to you. Plowsy was as honest a fellow when he commenced life, as I have no doubt you are yourself, and as cheerful and comfortable. At present, unless, I may be permitted to say, for me, where and what would he be ? "

Observing that I looked mystified, he went on : " Possibly you are not aware of the Millionaire Relief Agency Company (Limited), though I am both sorry and glad to say it is well known to most of our profession. When I settled down on my million, and had to decide on my vocation, I admonished myself : 'Ditchling, never forget that charity begins at home. You are now a millionaire, Ditchling, and millionaires are your first charge. Stick to your class. Your duty is to shed a little sunshine on their melancholy existence.' I have acted on that principle, and am thankful to think that I have not laboured wholly in vain.

"When I had formulated my plan, I called a meeting of millionaires and explained it. I appealed to the experience of many before me, on the comfortlessness of an existence separated by the unsympathetic barrier of a made million from all accustomed pleasures, pursuits, and associations. My idea was that a society should be founded, with a complete organization for the confidential inquiry into and relief of destitute cases. I proposed that there should be a body of private detectives, secretaries, patrons unpaid, and almoners, and that every full millionaire should be required to subscribe one guinea a year.

"The project, all except the last clause, which, however, was carried by a narrow majority, was welcomed enthusiastically. Officers were elected on the spot, I being chosen among the first almoners. We take the work week about, and this is my week. Necessarily, success is only a relative term. With a multitude to assist, and in miseries of the most aggravated and various types, one cannot do all. But we are perpetually at it, and we accomplish something. You can easily comprehend that I am not very comfortable when I hear

young men like you talk of becoming millionaires.
Our burden is enough as it is; we want no more on
our shoulders. The poor creatures, you see, have
merely learnt how to make their million. They
have not the least idea how to enjoy it. Often
they are in need of the barest comforts.

"You met me coming up the steps this evening
at 102, Grosvenor Square. I have had a long day
of it. Bless you! Number a hundred and two is
not the only house I had been visiting. I had been
to two others in the Square itself, and to a dozen
elsewhere. Distances are so long in London, and
millionaires live so far apart! Look at my visit-
ing-list for one day. Mayfair, five. That is easy;
all close together. Then, one in Maida Vale.
In Highbury, one. One on Denmark Hill, and
one in Russell Square. One, Mansion House, E. C.
All within the four miles' radius. I stipulated for
that. Even thus limited, what spaces to travel,
and with that laden bag to haul the whole round.

"When I started this morning it was too full
to shut close. I saw you found it load enough
when it was empty, or all but. Glance at my
way bill, and judge what it felt like before. Look;
at 102 in the Square there were the periwinkles
and pincushion, with three best silver-headed pins.
Old Grasgrene doats on periwinkles; romantic

early associations; wife's portrait; and his daughters will not let one come into the house if they
know it. I discovered that for which my excellent
friend was pining. I cheer his declining years by
stealing in with a pint twice a week in the season.
Then there are the *Family Heralds* for Mrs. Skeech.
They are the sole literature she cares for, and she
belongs to two Lady Clubs, and three fashionable
lending libraries, none of which take the *Herald*
in. Again, there are the skittles — dreadfully
heavy — for Jackson at his sumptuous Jackson-
ville in the Regent's Park. We put them up in his
American bowling-alley, and play, with the doors
locked, for a couple of hours.

"I should not so much mind the carpet-bag,
and the walking, and the skittles, and all that,
if it were not for the cross-questioning of the
patients. They are like dumb animals, and cannot articulately describe their privations. Sometimes they are ashamed to say. I live on the
back stairs, and in the kitchen, and area, in order
to find out. I have to catechise a man, and extract an entire autobiography, before the ailment
discloses itself. He does not know. He is clearly
out of sorts, body and mind. He has not the
vaguest notion of a cure. Money will not serve;
and it is the one thing he can think of.

"Off he goes and buys a park. Or he turns into Bond-street, and pays £5000 for an artist's model dressed up as the Woman of Samaria, and probably not much better in character. I have come upon a millionaire sitting before a cabinet of £10,000-worth of Sicilian coins, and with the air of expecting a call from the hangman. He had bought it because he felt a bit down, and his daughter had read out to him from the *Numismatic Gazette* that the medicine for a sore heart, the loss of a child or of an election, was a Queen Philistis stater. In a Leicester Square catalogue, he noticed a cabinet, which was described as having three. So he sent a blank bid, and got the lot.

"He had not been sure before whether a stater were not a stuffed alligator. When he knew, he was more depressed than ever. He believed himself incurable. 'The medicine, the one medicine,' he kept muttering in a dazed way. This is how I treated his case. I went straight to the kitchen, gave the man-cook — a Frenchman — a holiday to go to see Sarah Bernhardt, and sent to the public-house at the corner of the mews for a pot of porter. I toasted a rabbit myself, and took it and the porter upstairs. Down tumbled the stater, and my patient burst into tears. For many years he had not felt the touch of pewter. For the time he was a new man. Only it is a kind of remedy which has to be renewed pretty frequently.

"The particular panacea is not always so handy. Once I had to bring up half a dozen Poppleton-cum-Swipes coprolite poachers to gossip with a railway contractor who had begun life in that capacity, and was threatened with torpor numma-rius. My difficulty was that I had to send a confidential agent to Berlin to learn from the German General Staff where Poppleton-cum-Swipes is.

"If I felt free to sweep a man clean out of surroundings which are stifling him, I could generally cope with the specific disease. But it is kill or cure. I tried breaking a millionaire hypochondriac, with alarming results. Miserable as he had been on account of his possessions, he was worse without them. I had to put him in the way of accumulating a second million; and he was more wretched still. He kept dreaming of the things he might have done if he had but the original one besides. Experience has shown me it is wisest not to meddle with facts, unless to supplement them. The sole safe rule is to assume that a man's million will never be applied by him for anything he himself truly needs.

"But let us have some tea." He rang, and a tray was brought. Mr. Ditchling looked it over, and his face visibly fell. "No marmalade?" he asked the untidy maid-servant. "No, sir," she answered pertly; "don't you remember you eat the last this morning at breakfast, and you told me never to get in more than one jar a week." "Yes," he cried peevishly; "and plenty, if it were kept for me. It is the one thing I care for." In sorrow he left the room to search for the key of the tea-caddy. I caught up my hat, and ran round to a late general shop in the side street. I bought a jar, and was back before he had discovered his key. I placed it by the side of the tray. I fancied I saw a tear in his eye, and I said good-night, that he might have the undisturbed enjoyment both of his marmalade and of his emotion.

Now that I am acquainted with the existence of the Relief Agency and its objects, I come upon frequent traces of its benevolent mission. When you see a shabby old fellow with a bag slinking up or down the area steps of some Tyburnian, Belgravian, or Mayfair mansion in the dusk, you may be pretty sure it is one of the almoners of the M. R. A. (Limited) on his charitable round.

CHAPTER XVIII.

THE CLUB.

I HAVE cultivated Bugbrooke's society a good deal since I learnt what he was. There always is a little embarrassment in social relations when you are not aware of the nature of a friend's income. Lately I fell in with him in the neighbourhood of lunch time. I began walking with him towards Russell Square, before he casually mentioned that he had an engagement out. I had been joking him on his liking better to be spoken of as respectable than as a millionaire. But, as he reminded me, he had always said that he did not object to being known for the latter also. "If anybody," he very good-humouredly remarked, "be pleased to think me a millionaire, and spread it abroad, he is welcome. I am not like Brommage, who lives in a worse house, at the same rent, round the corner. He dare not live in the Square, for fear he should be accounted rich. You know Brommage. No? There he goes, sneaking away to lunch at his club. Ever been there? A nice lively place. You say you should be glad to go—

care to see varieties of life.   Ah! you don't know what you are in for.   Well, if you will, you will. Hi! Brommage.   Here is a friend of mine who wants a word with you.   Mr. Twygge — Mr. Brommage.   Ta-ta.   I have to arrange with my brother churchwarden, over a glass of madeira, how to turn St. Giles into Venetian-Gothic.   We shall head the subscription-list.   I know, Brommage, you can't afford to help us, except by stealth."

I was left with Mr. Brommage, who perplexed me.   I detected a wrinkle, though kept carefully ironed out, so as to look no more than a spectacle crease.   On the other hand, his dress!   Not the ostentatious millionaire's splendour, and not the disdainful millionaire's slovenliness.   His was the shabby, brushed gentility, as if a careful wife tried to keep him trim, which is not the habit of millionairesses.   His manner of speech, too, and his gestures, were timid and discreet.   He under-slid glances at me, which meant, not that he thought I was going to endeavour to borrow money from him — I am well acquainted with that millionaire look — but that he fancied I apprehended he was about to seek a small loan from me.   Probably he was not as aware as myself how perfectly safe, for an excellent reason, I knew my pocket to be.

At any rate, I determined to clear up any doubt. I said I saw we were walking in the same direction, and if he would allow me, we would walk together. With half an eye I could see that he wished me at Jericho, but had not the courage to say it. That, again, hindered me from feeling secure against imposture; for millionaires, shabby or smart, misers or misanthropes, rarely are shy of speaking their minds. However, we strolled on amicably enough, he, meanwhile, continuing to peep at me curiously. At last, when the ice, in the genial surroundings of Woburn Place, had a little melted, he burst out, almost involuntarily : " I wish to goodness, Mr. Twygge, you would let me know how you manage it." " Do what ?" I asked. " Hide it," he said. " Hide what ?" I repeated. " For twenty years," he proceeded, " I have been trying, and all at the Club have been trying, and we never quite succeed. Something will betray us. But I conceived I was conversant with every sign of a millionaire, and positively you show none. For charity come in, and tell our fellows. We shall be everlastingly grateful."

By this time we were in a passage running from Little Coram-street, and were standing in the mildewed fly-blown entry of a poverty-stricken house. On the lintel was the mystic inscription, " A. O.

Buffaloes, Div. Mill. Lodge 333. 6 Geo. iv. Ch. 92."
I was half-way up a dark staircase before I had the
presence of mind to mention that I was not a millionaire, at least as yet. It requires some courage
to say you are not, after you have been mistaken
for one. Mr. Brommage, who had turned bold
and cheerful as soon as the door closed, bore it
very pleasantly. "That is, indeed, a joke," he
cried. "But all my fault, or Bugbrooke's. In
general, our folks, you know, have no acquaintances outside. Other people are nasty-tempered,
and won't have us. I had forgotten about Bugbrooke's peculiarity. Is fond of knowing respectable persons, he says. Never mind, I have dragged
you here, and you lunch with me."

I could do no less than accept Mr. Brommage's
apology for his inadvertence. I inquired the name
of the Club, which, well out of range of envious
observation from without, was furnished solidly
and even handsomely, but still more comfortably.
"Of course," said Mr. Brommage, "in the Post
Office Directory it is a lodge of the Royal Ante-
diluvian Order of Ancient Buffaloes. You noticed
the letters over the street door. Its proper name
is French, given by the Paris R. ' les Millionnaires
honteux.' As not all of us speak French, we have
anglicized it among ourselves, indifferently, into
the Shymills or the Golden Moles."

Well, I willingly admit, the Moles lunch satisfactorily. Such a slice of salmon! Such four-year-old mutton! Such a glass of port! I made a mental note that I would lunch with them often. From the coffee-room we adjourned to a smoking-room. Seven or eight members were already there, smoking church-wardens of a peculiar make, and so vigorously that I could not easily see their faces. From the same cause they could not clearly observe mine, which, with '47 port at midday, may partly account for their failure to perceive that I was not one of themselves. My host had not concealed it. He stated the fact as he introduced me into the circle. Evidently he was not credited. His statement raised a little polite laugh. "So like a friend of Brommage's," I heard whispered. I was supposed to be only the better fitted for honorary membership of the Shymills. My comments on their talk and my questions for my own enlightenment, added, I saw, as the afternoon went on, to the general amusement. They were accepted as characteristically humorous.

It was an admirable opportunity for me, of which I fully availed myself. I was surprised and charmed to find how frank, among themselves, they all were. They wrap themselves in external mystery, only to be the more expansive and candid in the security of club life. Not, indeed, that I have much reason to complain of secretiveness on the part of millionaires to me, even out of doors. But then I cannot conceal from myself that, as probably I have already mentioned, I have a way with me.

Some casual incident led to it. I rather think a member, not thinking, was about to open a window on the street side, to let out a little of the smoke. Another warned him that we should be overlooked. At all events, I had an occasion for inquiring of a neighbour — a Mr. Skinflint, I heard — why they were all afraid to be recognized for what they were. His reply, off-hand, as if to an intentional paradox, was that they were ashamed. " You must acknowledge," said he, " though plenty do it, that it is rather a shabby thing to have got a million." " You mean," I asked, " because a man must have been a shade too clever, must have steered too near the wind ? " " What can that matter ? " he said. " No ; it is the money itself, the having it. To pick up a million is to put yourself on scavenger's work, which, if necessary, is not nice. Every millionaire, after all, is a sort of nightman. How should he have made his million if it were not muck ?

" Look at us. Is Jeek particularly brilliant ? I

am certain I am not. Robbs in the corner could
not spell without a dictionary, to save his life. As
we could not cajole briefs from attorneys, or write
magazine articles and novels, or paint portraits,
or wag our heads in pulpits, or job our way into
politics, we had to sweep up the millions. Somebody had to do it; and we are the somebodies.
When the world wants its money, it spends it,
breathes it into honest vapour. There's an end
of it till it is condensed back again. A £100 goes
here, a five-shilling piece, or a £1000 there.
But there is always a deal over messing about
under everybody's feet, more than enough to glut
markets, fill the gin palaces, spoil good artists,
writers, lawyers, and doctors. Without us to brush
up, the dust would be in everybody's throat. Not
a very pretty employment ours, perhaps. At least
it keeps a place tidy. If we are not always very
clean, it is that we have to clean up for the public.
It is too bad that we are so much disliked, though
it may be natural. I have read that they threw
bricks at the embalmers who scrubbed out the
fine Egyptian gentlemen's insides."

I assured the speaker that not all just and
liberal-minded paupers despised millionaires, to
which he only replied that a great many paupers are neither liberal-minded nor just. "We

were obliged," he went on, "to set up this little free-and-easy to have any society. Tiresome, no doubt, for us to be condemned to live with one another. Still, thick-headedness is more endurable than to have people looking as if there were something catching about you. Here we all have the itch, metaphorically speaking, and don't mind."

The rest had been listening to Mr. Skinflint's little dissertation, and for the most part murmured self-compassionating approval. One after another, however, urged, both that some persons must undertake the millionairing business, and that individual millionaires rarely had any option, whether in making or in spending. Mr. Smith, for example — Thomas Smith, it was explained to me, not John Smith, of Smith Bros. — represented forcibly the extent to which modern competition was responsible for the resort to the employment. He himself had been at a great commercial school, where he took every classical prize. He had, his tutor told him, all the world to choose from, and he set about choosing. Lost labour, he discovered. Bar, medicine, church, the press, engineering, the army, the fleet, — not an inch of space to thrust his nose in. He stood, on the strength of scholarship, for a Somerset House clerkship, and might as profitably have sent in his name for the archbishopric of Canterbury. Every single occupation was blocked, except money. So he apprenticed himself to the million-making. In that there always is room, for the right sort. The getting he thought not bad work. The worst was that his million came too soon ; and then he had to learn, from the first rudiments, how to lay it out.

He told a pitiful tale of the shifts and humiliations he had undergone in the endeavour to employ his income, which would keep washing, as it were, over him. A chorus of sympathetic assents from all sides testified to the reminiscences of experiences as sad, which his narrative evoked. Nearly every man in the room seemed able to match the chronicle. The singular form of destitution which afflicts the millionaire class appears to be constantly extending. All grades of public bodies, from country councils downwards, nowadays, I judged from the remonstrances uttered, have begun to compete with individual benefactors. One member spoke indignantly of a deputation, on which he had served the previous week, to the Treasury, to expostulate on the want of encouragement to millionaires. The Department, once so virtuously stingy, had been purchasing over the head of a millionaire syndicate, at the price of £57,555, the Leamington Titian. " Gentlemen," was the simple answer of the First Lord, who was accompanied by the Financial Secretary, to the reproach on the waste of public money: "Gentlemen, we must muddle it away somehow."

When a millionaire has secured the concession of an expensive idea, and works it, he can never be sure, as one member after another confessed with sorrow, that the good he does may not have a reverse side to it. I do not myself know how that is. I only listened to various enterprises in which members of the club are at present engaged, and I thought them most benevolent and interesting. That is my common inclination of mind on the subject of the acts of millionaires.

Mr. Migge said he was having the area rails in Somers-town gilt for the sake of the inculcation of sweetness and light. The mission of Mr. Dredge, who confesses he may have caught the idea from Mr. Barstrow, is the explosion of obsolete institutions. They call him the Grave-digger at the Charity Commission. Last year he compelled an inquiry into the Ramillies Wig Almhouses, a set of comfortable, new Queen Anne villas, tenanted by six gentlemen, and an equal number of maiden ladies. He elicited that all the gentlemen and three of the ladies wore their own hair. An appeal to the Lords on the question whether the past can be condoned by a clean shave is now pending.

Mr. Jones, again, for the sake of occupation, has retained a herald, who is demonstrating for him the blood relationship of all of his name. A well-known genealogical metaphysician is reported to be awaiting with intense anxiety the incidental solution of the moot question whether every Jones part his hair in a line deviating from that which marks the lineage of the Browns.

Mr. Groundsell is having the private history of preachers, philanthropists, and patriots compiled by a staff of private detectives. His object is to ascertain whether it be an invariable rule, or merely a common accident, that persons with a high standard for others are low livers for themselves. He wants to know, he says.

Mr. Doublerepps, every afternoon, except in December, which he passes at Margate, drives through the East End in a Victoria, with a £10 note loose on the footboard. A mounted secretary attends, whose duty it is to follow the note, as soon as a gust carries it off, and track the finder for the next three days. Mrs. Doublerepps, who is writing on Original Sin, desires to ascertain whether windfalls work good or ill.

Mr. Ezekiel Brickdust supplies the Sunday-school children in Evangelical churches through July with patent noiseless ginger-beer. The rest of the year and of his surplus dividends he spends in replanting with dandelions the country roads, which have been stripped in consequence of the choice of that flower by an eminent statesman for his vegetable emblem. Isaac Brickdust, a rare instance of a second millionaire in the same family, has bathing trains to Worthing, Herne Bay, and Littlehampton every week in August, for the street Arabs. He selects by preference the most dust-dried and dirt-caked. His pleasure is to see them return in the evening with a surface of real skin. By arrangement with him, Mr. George Grossmith, Mr. Corney Grain, and Mr. Toole perform gratuitously on the previous evenings in those three gay resorts, in order that the demeanour of the regular residents may not be too dispiriting to the temporary visitors.

Finally, Mr. Squaretos, or Dot-and-Go-One, as he used to be termed in his præ-millionaire days, told us how he accepts, to the extent of £40,000 a year, an allotment in every new company which promises not less than twenty-five per cent. He says his aim is to save the widows and orphans from that amount of pillage.

The club is, as I have mentioned, limited. All

members must reside in the West Central district. Other Postal divisions have similar institutions for their millionaires. This one is restricted to one hundred and fifty ordinary members, of whom scarcely more than a fifteenth part happened to be in the smoking-room. Almost all had propounded, and, apparently, were in the habit of practising, ways of disbursing very considerable sums of money. I have no reason to doubt that every absent member is at least as thoughtful for the community, and as bountiful. My imagination almost reeled before the panorama of all these benefactors of humanity labouring, first at raking in their millions, and then pouring them forth broadcast on the commonalty.

Taking simply as samples the modes of expenditure which had been described, I felt more in love than ever with the chivalrous calling. Could there be more ingeniously noble applications of large means? As I heard each scheme unfolded, I was suffused with admiration almost to an uncomfortable degree. Yet the public benefactors themselves spoke apologetically, as if they were on their defence against a charge of qualifying for Hanwell. They are too sensitively conscientious for their own happiness. One of the strangest phenomena I have observed in millionaires is the tendency to a sudden and abnormal growth of conscience. While they are on their probation, and are struggling upwards to their lofty dignity, I know no men who have a heartier contempt for morbid scruples about money-making. As soon as they have arrived, a cell opens in their brain, and they become scrupulosity incarnate. If the effect were merely to induce them to button up their pockets, I could understand and applaud their respect for the precious contents. But their consciences have a habit of criticising after the money has found an outlet, with the result that they render men who seem to me to be the salt of the earth often exceedingly miserable.

This is why, though I could not at all approve of the levity of references to persons of untold wealth, and to their money itself, I must admit that I listened with some pleasure to the remarks of Mr. Towzles on his millionaire brethren's inordinate addiction to self-tormenting. All through, I had noticed Mr. Towzles, the most timid of millionaires outside the Club, but a very brave one within, venting his disagreement with most which was being said in a series of snorts — the millionaire snort, not the parish vestryman's. At length he could restrain himself no longer.

"I wonder," he burst out, " whether you fellows

be more of fools or hypocrites. Not a man of you has said a sensible thing, except Skinflint; and he has got hold of the wrong end of the stick. I am not scolding you for your playing at charity or justice. On the contrary, I think you much more honest than Rattletrap, who starves himself, in order to leave three millions instead of two to his unknown next of kin. At least, you consider that they who have had the pleasure of making the pile should bear the burden of scattering it. You do not shuffle off your responsibility upon others. But the nonsense is to complain of the money for crowding in upon you, or to fancy it matters what becomes of it when it drops out of your strong boxes.

"You go about as self-important as a hen with the pip, pondering whether you have done well or ill in spending in this way or in that. Spend, and you can't be wrong. A mission, indeed! The obligations of riches! Do you imagine we are likely persons to have been chosen for trustees of millions, if the millions cared what was done with them? Whenever the world has, as often, money it does not need and cannot properly distribute, it creates a millionaire for its own convenience. You say I have no respect for money? I beg your pardon; only it has no respect for me.

Money knows its way about better than you and I. Before it thought of coming to us it had become a bit tired and out of sorts, or had been pushed by a playmate off the course. Then it has said to itself: 'Drat it all! I'm a surplus; I'll have a sleep,' and it crowds into pockets like yours and mine, like a pet squirrel. Your delusion is that it wants your advice, that it wants to be done good with. The absurdity! It came to yawn and snore, and play antics with its own tail. The instant it has recovered its spirits off it scurries, whether from the till of the Conger Eel Protection Society's secretary, or from the purse of your residuary legatee, to be virtuously busy and useful. Money is not a baby; the babies are you who offer to put it in leading-strings, and are afflicted if it insist upon tumbling about.

" What is my own receipt, you ask, for the disposal of refuse? Oh! I am no cleverer than the rest of you. I keep a secretary to read the end leaders in the morning papers. I suspect she sometimes writes them. They are always admonishing millionaires what to do with their spare cash, and I take their advice. Since I adopted that method I have very seldom had any trouble with bloated balances. Am I not occasionally

imposed upon? Constantly; and what were millionaires made for, except to be imposed upon?
A millionaire who just lays his carcass out in his
Tower of Silence, for the birds of prey to scream
over, and clutch, and tear to pieces, and bear away
to the four quarters of the globe, is accomplishing
his destiny least harmfully. That's what Towzles
thinks."

CHAPTER XIX.

THE CI-DEVANT.

I LEFT the Club with my host. A gentleman to whom I had not been introduced was putting on his coat in the passage, and went out with us. Both in the coffee and smoking rooms he had attracted my attention by neither lunching, nor smoking, nor talking. He appeared to count the cost of every mouthful of food and smoke, and to drink in every word. He was old or elderly and better dressed than are millionaires in general. There was, and there was not, the millionaire look on his countenance, the satiety look. The more habitual expression seemed to be that of a man-eater, when the noble creature has shed its teeth and claws. He was in advance as we issued into Little Coram-street, and I asked in a low voice who or what he was. "You mean the Ci-devant; the wretchedest being on earth," was Mr. Brommage's reply; "do not talk of him; he gives me the shudders." The natural answer to such an invitation was to talk of him, and I began to interrogate. "Well," said Brommage, "if you want to make yourself uncomfortable, you are welcome. But you will have to do it by yourself."

We hastened our steps and overtook the stranger, who was walking listlessly on, with his eyes on the ground, like Mammon's. A few conventional remarks on the weather, the Mincing Lane markets, the Deceased Wife's Sister Bill, and the like, took us to one of the connecting streets between Russell and Bedford Squares, where Brommage resides. At that point Brommage, as he mounted his doorstep, which was characteristically mouldy, introduced me to Mr. Deunce, as his acquaintance was named. "Not of ours at present," he observed of me aside to Mr. Deunce; "but training, I believe, for it." "Let him be a tinker rather," cried Mr. Deunce, aloud. "The most ungrateful profession on earth!" "Ah!" said Brommage, "if you be going to warn him, I must be off."

I proceeded with Mr. Deunce, who stopped soon before the door of an excellent, old-fashioned house in Bedford Square. As I waited till the door was opened, by a man in sober livery, Mr. Deunce invited me to continue our conversation in his very well-appointed study. Under pressure, I accepted. I lost no time in inquiring the reasons for his aversion from the millionaire call-

ing.   I suggested he meant that money palls upon
its possessors.   He said he was not such an idiot;
that the danger of which he was thinking was
the torment of having had, and having it no
longer.   "I had my million, young man," he said,
"and I have it not.   Look at me, and beware."

"Yes," after a pause he resumed, "painfully and
skilfully, with unprecedented good fortune to aid,
I climbed to the top of the pole.   I had my re-
verses, and back had fallen a dozen times before
arriving.   Half as many times I was ruined outright, and the world never knew.   Gaily I recommenced over and over again, and reached the old
point, and a point beyond.   You may slip safely
at £100,000, at £200,000, at £950,000, and start
afresh, with all your nerve.   I did.   At last there
it was, my million; and I folded my hands, to be
happy.

"Alas!   Browns and I had graduated in the
same 'In Mill. Stud.' Tripos.   We entered upon
life on even terms.   But he had the luck to die
as early as sixty-three, and be proved for two millions sterling.   The paragraph stared me in the
face — two clear millions; and I, at least his
match for brains and audacity, had just turned
one.   A man of spirit could never stand that, and
I had to return to the oakum-picking.   Not a pleas-

ant prospect; for that is all stuff which Smith was saying about the delight of making, and the nuisance of spending. Three weeks of millionaire-crotcheteering showed me how heavenly it is. Just three weeks. Only five days before I had been balloted into the Club; and I had not yet disposed of the money-grubbery. So, I put my head back into the halter once more. Of course, I see now that I must have been demented to try it. Nothing is strange in my catastrophe, unless the insanity of the victim. I had my spring, and seized my million. It was not to be done a second time. Three weeks before, I had the instinct fresh and keen. I had it when I was eighteenpence short of the round sum. It had fulfilled its duty, and it took its discharge for good.

"Browns himself, you remind me, at my age was worth a couple of millions. Yes; but he had never made up his capital account; he had not lain down to maul, and devour, and digest. Troops of other millionaires, you say, years after they have attained full rank, have their pile doubled, trebled, quintupled. Yes; but not by them. They slumber, and the ball rolls itself along, and swells. For that I had too much vitality, and I dared to do work for which I had too little. I was in a hurry to be certain that I should equal Browns whenever my time came.

"I bought up all the futures in the market. In happier hours, cotton would thereupon have obediently jumped a halfpenny a pound. Now it dropped three farthings when I had to realize; sugar the same; grease and crude petroleum the same; Dahomey teeth — finest Amazons — no better; babies' corals the same. Not by big sums, but by five thousands and ten thousands, my positive million melted, melted, melted! At every touch of my anxious, feverish fingers something thawed off. Was there ever a more tragical fate than mine? Napoleon's in Russia? But mine was a veritable million of pounds sterling, not of human rubbish. By the end of three deadly years, when I had satisfied my liabilities, I stood a pauper.

"You say I do not look a pauper; that you would suppose I spent an income of a couple of thousands? That's my wife's settlement, and those brutes, her trustees, though I feel I have recovered my instinct, will not let me have the petty capital to multiply twentyfold. You ask how much I was accustomed to spend formerly. Not that; I have a right to say certainly not that. Oh! I see what you are driving at. But there was good in saving then, none now. 'Scatter, squander,' I repeat to my wife from morning to night; 'and let us die in the gutter.' You should have thought it practicable, you say, to live agreeably on £2000 a year, without a million? Perfectly; but it is not practicable to have had your million and lost it, and be content. I sit, I tell you, and dream here of all I was to have done with my million, or might have done. There is so much spending in a million; and, above all, if you do not spend! There are so many visions in it! I see the hundreds of thousands marching up and up to some celestial portal. A door opens wide, and in they go, my hundreds of thousands, and I may not enter. I catch a gleam, I hear a pulsation of triumphal music; the gate shuts; and I am in darkness, silence, cold, and despair.

"I shall live, I feel, to be old, and am condemned to go on existing without my million. To think of the long years I shall survive to be pitied by such as Pogson, and Gregson, and Brommage, and Diddler; to be a retired member of the Club of which I ought to be Grand Chamberlain, licensed to eat and drink and smoke, but not to pay; to listen silently to others comparing notes on their delicious gambols, and fancy vainly how it is in me to have been as crazy as the craziest; to foresee that on my tombstone will never be writ, 'Here lies John Deunce, Mill.'!"

He scowled at me, with a glittering eye, but as

blackly as if the modest inscription had been filched from him for the unfair and premature embellishment of my grave. I bade him adieu rather in haste. As I caught sight of him over my shoulder in the chimney glass, he was grimacing and mowing like one of Hogarth's figures in Bedlam.

CHAPTER XX.

I DO not deny that Mr. Deunce's tragical experiences and sinister warnings cast a lugubrious
shadow over my mind. Commencing my studies
of millionaires as a matter purely of literary interest, I am conscious that gradually I have been
contracting a habit of meditating whether I should
not join the profession myself. In the first place,
I have now invested a tidy capital in the subject.
Millionaires cannot be said to be amusing companions. They are not gifted with the talent of society. They are dull and heavy. They are apt to
be rude. They are not liberal, unless to their own
particular crotchets. After one has been steeped
in familiar intercourse with them for a year or
more, one does not put up readily with the idea
that it has been all for nothing. Moreover, there
are difficulties in the way of relapsing into middle-
class financial companionship, where one is apt to
offend by casual references to something superior.

I am sensible, too, I confess, of a certain fascination, if not in millionaires, in millions. A million is so extraordinarily self-sufficing. Even a mean million of francs is not without the charm, which obviously is increased twenty, or five and twenty, fold, with several centimes over, when the million is sterling. The defect — as from some points of view it clearly is, that one cannot handle, and can scarcely count, a million with existing senses, which, it may be humbly hoped, will be hereafter enlarged for the purpose — is from other points an enhancement of its merits. It can be thought of around and around, without the friction to the brain of being brought up short with a bump at the end. With a million to roll about in the fancy, like a quid of tobacco in the cheek, no other mental occupation is needed. It is food alike for the moral and the intellectual qualities.

A question between the rival dividend-earning powers of gas and electricity warms and illuminates right through. Like electricity, not in the Capel Court sense, it fills up all the gaps. In company with a million, it is possible to wander about a boundless Paradise, and never be far away from home. If the sermon be long, Grand Trunks will outstay it. If your mistress be tart, the great Devon Consols will sweeten existence. All degrees of intelligence are equal to the topic of

money, and none are above it. I agree with the
Great Grimsby, not the fish emporium, that for
the purposes of solid ambition in quest of posthu-
mous influence and fame, give me the Paddington
or Euston register. Tie yourself to scores of thousands substantially invested, and you are safe to
slide merrily on, outside the realms of eternal
oblivion. Enshrined in a cutting from the *Illustrated London News*, you will not all die. Though
French or Germans were marching up Ludgate
Hill to beard the Lord Mayor, that would be read.
What is a blue or brass oval on a poet's or
romancer's middle-class tenement to a favourable
notice in Wills and Bequests? Ask the Chancel-
lor of the Exchequer which he deems the worthier
citizen, the writer with a will proved under £1000,
or an oil-man with £1,000,000? Which dust
smells more sweetly?

When a millionaire retires finally from business,
he mounts a triumphal car, and he does not with-
draw before the curtain falls. That is a mark
of the delightfulness of the vocation. Its members have no desire for interminable holidays.
They often say they have given up. I have been
obliged, by my duties, to watch them narrowly,
and I know better. I have generally met them
the next morning entering the office of their pri-

vate stockbrokers. They talk of the joys of leisure. They harangue on the satisfaction of parting with their pelf. Catch them without a whistle among their watch-charms to summon it back.

I appreciate sincerely these virtues of a million, especially the solace, grateful yet not unwholesomely exciting, which it affords, against the tedium of a superfluous half-hour at a railway station. The millionaire pursuit also has the advantage of being one in which success is comparatively easy. Few young men have a right to expect to be Bishops, Royal Academicians, Editors, Medical Baronets, Lord Chancellors, or even Lords Justices. Any steady, shrewd, industrious, sober, well-conducted lad may determine to end as a millionaire. On the whole, if he have no really respectable occupation in view, he is wise to determine.

Very many adopt the calling. I ought to know as I compile the list, which follows that of Milliners-stand-makers. It has added considerably to the bulk of Kelly's Trades Directory. Lengthy as it is, it is nothing like what it would be if all the members of Millionaire Clubs were included. Most manage to escape notice by never filling up an Income Tax paper. Their companies in which their hundreds of thousands are invested save them

from the exposure. Before I had cultivated the eye
for them I passed them by the score without recog-
nizing them. Now, I see them everywhere. They
always keep on the kerb, where they run only
half the danger of having their pockets picked.
For their convenience the Commissioners of Sewers
in the City have set the lamp-posts back, so that
they may walk straight on. An afternoon or
two ago I was trying to cross to Cornhill. In the
little crowd waiting with me I counted eight,
beside one who edged himself among them,
though, to my certain knowledge, he has hardly
half the money. Five of the eight went with me
into Birch's for their usual lunch, four maids of
honour, and a puff. The ninth, the mock turtle,
passed through to the back shop, and ordered a
plate of real. I saw the five nudge one another.
The other three were taking the opportunity of
the sherry-and-biscuit hour to call on two insurance secretaries and a bank manager.

Certainly, the business has to be learnt, like
other trades; and all these good people, dunces
as they may be thought by the uninitiated, must
have some ability for it. Still, how few trades
there are in which so little of a regular apprenticeship must be served! All sorts of waifs and
strays, the bad sixpences of other pursuits, drift

into it and prosper.   Not to speak of testamentary
millionaires, whom any Grimsby can manufacture
offhand — out of myself, for example, provided
he do not forget to bequeath enough over to cover
legacy duty — the fact is that the art at first hand
is ridiculously easy.   There is no occasion to attend, as I have, the Overstone course on million-
making at the Royal Institution.   The lecturer
enumerates so many different specifics that I have
known students fall into a downright quandary,
and be ordered off to Monte Carlo to clear their
brains.   The most practical working millionaires
can themselves tell a candidate little which he
could not have discovered as well for himself.
They are not surly when they are sure that one
is not wanting to borrow five shillings.   They
will communicate all the knowledge they possess
on the way to matriculate at their college.   But it
does not amount to more than that it is requisite
to have a surplus, and to invest it.

Mr. Grimsby put the whole philosophy of the
thing in a nut-shell for me one afternoon: "You
find your £100,000, or if you be, as I never was,
in a hurry, your £200,000.   You place your money
where it will make you three per cent, four, five,
six, ten per cent; that's just as it happens.   You
live on your £600 a year; what more can a man

spend? I never spent so much. The rest you put where your first was, or anywhere else as advantageously. The first rule of arithmetic shows how it is done. Do it on a slate, and you will see how long a million takes to grow."

There is nothing more to add; for I asked Mr. Grimsby: "How about the first £100,000 you speak of?" His answer was given in a moment: "Confound you, Sir! you must begin somewhere!" At the moment, I acknowledge, the remark appeared to me more trenchant than argumentative. On consideration, however, I have perceived that the principle is the same, whatever the accidental amount of the surplus. The essential point is to have a surplus, little or big. It may be objected, I am aware, that some persons have no surplus. Granted. I should go even further, and say that most persons have none. Till they have, they have not the slightest chance of becoming millionaires. But that is because they choose not to join the class. If they say they cannot have a surplus, they talk nonsense. Everybody can have a surplus. If he have ten shilling a week, and exist upon it, he might exist upon nine and elevenpence halfpenny. There his margin is, and it will expand.

It is much easier to grow an indefinitely

increasing margin than an indefinitely increasing deficit. Try to live upon ten shillings and a halfpenny a week with an income of ten shillings. In time, according to arithmetic, you would be a million on the wrong side. Yet you never find that happen. Society, with its butchers and bakers, pulls you up abruptly; it allows no unlimited discretion in deficits. Has it ever been known to pull up a man because he notoriously is saving in order to grow his million? For all society cares, he may, and sometimes does, amass a dozen millions. In a more favourable hemisphere he has made forty. Prudent investments manifestly are essential. But there again abstruse philosophy is not necessary. Just buy cheap and sound, and sell dear and rotten. Whenever I set to at million-making I shall save sixpences first, and pounds afterwards. I have worked it all out by the help of a ready reckoner; with the compound interest.

There we have the broad and essential elements of the art of million-making, which experience will in various ways supplement and develop. Thus, not a bad method, after one has in hand the first £20,000, is, I am told, to borrow from a bank at four per cent and invest at five or six. Only care has to be taken that it is not the other way round, as the calculation is then altogether spoilt. To insure against disappointing surprises, the borrower should be clever at guessing whether the Bank of England be intending to alter its rate of discount.

At all events, after a really round sum has been collected, an intending millionaire may go to sleep. He should keep reasonable hours, and not play tricks with his digestion. It is well to have a good Government pension, not so much for the emoluments, though they are useful as subsistence money, as to make the pensioner feel that he has to go on revolving with the wheel of affairs. The mass of his money he ought to put into substantial securities not liable to spasmodic changes. A spare sum of £100,000 or so should be held in Gas or Water, in order to buy when a cry against either is raised, and to sell on the report of another grand purchasing scheme.

There is one little question on which I have the pain of reporting a variance of opinion between two eminent authorities, Pyncher and Mr. Grimsby. Mr. Grimsby, it may be recollected, is for cultivating an ideal of round quantities. He buys fractions with a distinct view to completing them. Pyncher, a cooler head, though without Mr. Grimsby's inspiration, is persuaded it is a weakness. I must confess that Pyncher's reasoning seems to me cogent, though I am sensible myself of the attraction. I am afraid that, when I had purchased £43,750 London & North-Western low after the launch of the Midland project for a crow-flight route between London and Liverpool, I should be very likely to be uneasy till I had bought the other £6250 at an exorbitant figure after the disallowance of the line by the House of Lords. But, as Pyncher says, it is a mistake to imagine that in investments there is "the other" this or that. Rounds are angles in finance, and angles are rounds. Every good investment has the quality of a diamond which will cleave into nothing but crystals, all equally perfect.

I have experienced personally the danger from the temptation, reprobated by Pyncher, to integrate fractions. Once I held, through a legacy, three Crystal Palace Ordinary shares, and I was not happy till, to round them, I had bought seven more out of my own money. Pray where is my money now? Good million-making stuff, in the shape, for instance, of £102,337 10 new Consols, associates itself on the best of terms with as sound, or nearly as sound, £79,252 Chatham and Dover Arbitration Debentures. Though a frayed coat will not go well with a new silk hat, the most dissimilar atoms of substantial securities fuse their dividends in one's bank pass-book as amiably as globules of quicksilver blend when they are shaken together. I am resolved they shall not quarrel in mine when I begin to despatch them thither.

Now I know it will be asked, " What then ? " I have, as I have explained, accommodated myself so completely to the society of millionaires as to be unfitted for any other. I have avowed that I am fonder still of the company and of the thought of millions. I have demonstrated by the indifference of the capacity of the practitioners and their abundance, that the profession is readily entered. I have proved that I have mastered the intricacies of the science, and have determined in advance, for myself, my rules of investment and accumulation. All this being so, it is, I admit, not unreasonable for persons — my able editor, for example — less experienced, perspicacious, and provident than myself to be impatient, according to their lights, at my delay in starting upon million-making forthwith. I am the more indisposed to complain of their criticisms, that to myself the still hypothetical question of beginning constitutes a puzzling enigma of idiopsychology. I am personally curious to know whether and when I am going to commence, and why I hold back.

So far as I can make out, after a minute process of self-examination, I do not believe that my hesitation is connected materially with the shade of depression caused in me by the Ci-devant's growls. Undoubtedly it is disagreeable to think that one may lose a million as well as make it. Perhaps the prospect is more peculiarly disagreeable for a person like myself who, not having yet made it, has necessarily been unable to enjoy its sweets. It is too bad to suffer the vexation of looking forward to the deprivation of a thing which I have never had the compensatory pleasure of possessing.

However, though my nature inclines me to look ahead, I do not think I could seriously be induced to abandon a promising career on account of a contingency which must be admitted to be, for the present, vague. Besides, as I should, when a millionaire, rigidly adhere to my infallible receipt for letting my money double and treble itself automatically, I incur no grave risk of undutiful desertion by my first million. If I understand myself at all, I believe my reluctance to set actively to work at money-making relates less to the chance of a calamity like Mr. Deunce's than to the apparent necessity of the opposite difficulty, the interminable accumulation. It is a formidable prospect, I allow, that making one million is a logical prelude to making two, and so forth to infinity. Never to be able to slip my neck out of the collar, or even into a different collar! Never a holiday from piling up the gold! Always to see the bunch of carrots in front of my doomed nose!

Still that itself might not be wholly unbearable if I could with confidence expect to be able to vary my exercise on the treadmill with frolics of expenditure, which, if not always very efficacious, evidently are most diverting. But I have seen enough of the millionaire life to know that there is not nearly a sufficient supply of such pastimes. All the available paradoxes are engaged far in advance; and I should have to wait my turn. Here, then, I am strongly inclined to suspect, is my secret but true stumbling-block and night-mare, odd as such a reason for rejecting a million must appear to less finely balanced natures.

It is astonishing indeed what perplexities disclose themselves in subjects apparently the most simple as soon as they are definitely and intelligently ap-proached. No employment could have been sup-posed to be more prosaically plain than spending. I have never myself found the least inconvenience in it on the scale on which I have commonly had to practise it. Apply it to a million, and one is at

once in the centre of a nest of hornets. I sometimes question, so acutely do I feel the overwhelm-
ing obligation of precise and accurate knowledge
of its destination before my million is made,
whether I shall ever consent to undertake the
preliminary task. It is a pity, as, for that, I am
convinced I have a talent. I cannot be such an
impostor as Snaggey, or such a blockhead as Diddler. But better an unmade million than a lost
millionaire!

The danger is that by some rash stroke of
financial genius I may prematurely compromise
my future and be forced to go and take my million because I have educated myself to know how.
For the present, at any rate, I feel tolerably safe.
My bank balance was under £20 last week, and
I shall be careful that next week it is less.

Meanwhile, for the sake of keeping my hand in,
I prosecute my survey of the field I am, I hope or
fear, fated hereafter to occupy, though my studies
are conducted under a slight temporary disadvan-
tage. The West Central Club has moved from
Little Coram-street, and left no address. This is
the more surprising as, when I was last a guest,
every member there pressed me to drop in as often
as I could, and to use his name to the steward. I
promised I would. Nobody hinted at a coming

migration.   Yesterday, after the decent interval of a short week, when I chanced promiscuously to pass, intending to ask for Smith or Towzles, I read "To let" chalked on the deliberately un-cleaned windows.   I had just before seen the same inscription in print on Brommage's resi-dence.   The whole clubhouse seemed empty and dilapidated.   I rapped at the door, which was opened captiously by an old woman in charge. "What?" asked I with diplomatic vagueness. "Sold up for rent," said she, and slammed to the door.   "Is not that," I ejaculated as I walked away, "the millionaires all over?"

Typography by J. S. Cushing & Co., Boston.